"I want you, Jane—"

She pulled sharply away from him. "You can't have me, Gabe," she told him dully. "Because I don't want you. I realize it must be difficult for the eligible Gabriel Vaughan to accept that a woman may not want him—"

"Cut the insults, Jane," he put in scathingly. "I heard what you said the first time around! What is it about you, Jane?" he added. "I've wanted you from the first moment I set eyes on you!"

CAROLE MORTIMER was born in England, the youngest of three children. She started writing in 1978, and has now written over 100 books for Harlequin Presents®.

Carole has four sons—Matthew, Joshua, Timothy and Peter—who keep her on her toes. She is very happily married to Peter, Sr. They live on the Isle of Man.

Carole Mortimer

A YULETIDE SEDUCTION

HARLEQUIN®

TORONTO • NEW YORK • LONDON
AMSTERDAM • PARIS • SYDNEY • HAMBURG
STOCKHOLM • ATHENS • TOKYO • MILAN • MADRID
PRAGUE • WARSAW • BUDAPEST • AUCKLAND

ISBN 0-373-12141-5

A YULETIDE SEDUCTION

First North American Publication 2000.

Copyright © 1999 by Carole Mortimer.

in U.S.A.

CHAPTER ONE

GOLD.

Bright, shiny, *tarnished* gold.

She didn't want to touch it any more than she needed to, didn't want it touching her either, the metal seeming to burn her flesh where it nestled on her left hand.

She pulled the gold from her finger. It wasn't difficult to do. She was so much slimmer than when the ring had first been placed on her finger. In fact, the ring had become so loose that it had spun loosely against her skin, only her knuckles stopping it from falling off by itself.

How she wished it had fallen off, fallen to the ground, never to be seen again. She should have pulled it off, wrenched it from her finger, weeks ago, months ago, but she had been consumed with other things. This tiny scrap of gold lying in the palm of her hand hadn't seemed important then.

But it was important now. It was the only physical reminder she had that she had ever—ever—

Her fingers closed around the small ring of metal, so tightly that her nails dug into her flesh, breaking through the skin. But she was immune to the pain. She even welcomed it. Because that slight stinging sensation in her hand, the show of blood, told her that she, at least, was still real. Everything around her seemed to have crumbled and fallen apart, until there was nothing left. She was the only reality, it seemed.

And this ring.

5

She unclenched her fingers, staring down at the ring, fighting back the memories just the sight of it evoked. Lies. All lies! And now he was dead, as dead as their marriage had been.

Oh, God, no! She wouldn't cry. Never that. Not again. Not ever again!

She quickly blinked back those tears before they could fall. Remember. She had to remember, to keep on remembering, before she would be allowed to forget! If she ever did...

But first she had to get rid of this ring. She never wanted it near her again, never wanted to set eyes on it again, or for anyone else to do so either.

Her fingers curled around it again, but lightly this time, and she lifted up her arm, swung it back as far as it would go, before launching it forward again. And as she did so she threw the ring as far as it would go, as far away from her as she could make it fly, watching as it spun through the air in what seemed like slow motion, making hardly a ripple in the water as it was swallowed up by the swiftly running river in front of her, falling down, to be sucked in by the mud and slime at the bottom of the river.

It took her several breath-holding seconds to realise it had gone. Finally. Irrevocably. And with its falling came release, freedom, a freedom she hadn't known for such a long, long time.

But freedom to do what...?

CHAPTER TWO

'TAKE the cups through to—' Jane abruptly broke off her calm instruction as one of those cups landed with a crash on the kitchen floor, its delicate china breaking into a dozen pieces. The three women in the room stared down at it, with the one who had dropped it looking absolutely horrified at what she had done.

'Oh, Jane, I'm so sorry.' Paula groaned her dismay. 'I don't know what happened. I'll pay for it, of course. I—'

'Don't be silly, Paula,' Jane dismissed, still calmly.

Once upon a time—and not so long ago—an accident like this would have sent Jane into a panic, the money she would have to pay for the replacement cup cutting deeply into the profit she would make from catering a private dinner party. But those days were gone now, thank goodness. Now she could afford the odd loss without considering it a disaster. Besides, if this evening was the success Felicity Warner hoped it would be, then Jane doubted the other woman would be too concerned that one of the coffee cups in her twelve-place-setting dinner service had met with an accident.

'Take the cups through.' Jane replaced the broken cup, putting it carefully beside the other seven already on the tray. 'Rosemary will bring the coffee. I'll clear away the broken cup.' She gave Paula's arm a reassuring squeeze before the two women left the high-tech kitchen to serve coffee to the Warners and their six dinner guests.

Jane almost laughed at herself as she bent down, dustpan and brush in her hand. In the last two years since she'd first begun this exclusive catering service to the rich and influential, she had moved from a one-woman band to being able to employ people like Paula and Rosemary to help with the serving, at least. But, nonetheless, she was back down on her hands and knees sweeping up! Some things just never changed!

'My dear Jane, I just had to— Darling...?' Felicity Warner herself had come out to the kitchen, coming to an abrupt halt as she spotted Jane on the floor behind the breakfast-bar. 'What on earth—?'

Jane straightened, holding out the dustpan containing the broken cup. 'You'll be reimbursed, of course—'

'Don't give it another thought, darling,' her employer for the evening dismissed uninterestedly, the affectation sounding perfectly natural coming from this elegantly beautiful woman, slim in her short, figure-hugging dress, long red hair loose about her shoulders, beautiful face alight with pleasure. 'After this evening I'm hoping to be able to buy a whole new dinner service and throw this old thing away!'

'This old thing' was a delicate china dinner service that would have cost thousands to buy rather than hundreds! 'It's been a success, then?' Jane queried politely as she disposed of the broken cup, her movements as measured and controlled as they usually were.

'A success!' Felicity laughed happily, clapping her hands together in pleasure. 'My dear Jane, after the wonderful meal you've served us this evening, Richard is likely to divorce me and marry you!'

Jane's professional smile didn't waver for a second, although inwardly the mere thought of being married to anyone, even someone as nice as Richard Warner appeared to be, filled her with revulsion. Although she knew Felicity was only joking; her husband obviously adored her and their two young daughters.

But she was pleased the evening seemed to be working out for this friendly couple. Cooking this evening's meal for the Warners had been a last-minute arrangement, aided by the fact that Jane had had a cancellation in her busy diary. And, from what Felicity had told her this afternoon, the last few months had been difficult ones for her husband's business. The couple could certainly do with a little good luck for a change!

Although it was the first time Jane had actually cooked for Felicity, she had found the other woman warm and friendly; in fact, the other woman had been chattering away to her all afternoon. Some of it through nervousness concerning the success of this evening, Jane was sure, and so she had just let Felicity talk as she continued to work.

Every morsel of food that had appeared on the table this evening had been personally prepared by Jane herself, even down to the chocolates now being served with the coffee, meaning that she'd spent a considerable time at her client's home before the meal was due to begin. Felicity, aware of how important this evening was—to her husband, to the whole family—had followed Jane about the kitchen most of the afternoon, talking endlessly. So much so that Jane now felt she knew the family—and their problems—intimately. Felicity obviously felt the same way!

'Nothing has actually been said, of course,' Felicity continued excitedly. 'But Gabe has asked to meet Richard at his office tomorrow morning, so that they can "talk".' She smiled her pleasure at this development. 'A vast improvement on just buying Richard out and to hell with him! And I'm sure it's your wonderful meal that's mellowed him and tipped the balance!' She grinned conspiratorially. 'He told me he doesn't usually eat dessert, but I persuaded him to just try a little of your wonderful white chocolate mousse—and there wasn't a word out of him while he ate every mouthful! He was so relaxed by the time he had eaten it that he readily agreed to talk with Richard in the morning!' she concluded gleefully.

So it wasn't the other man who had actually asked for the meeting, but Richard Warner who had instigated it. Oh, well, a little poetic licence was allowed on the other woman's part in the circumstances. Felicity's husband ran and owned an ailing computer company, and, from what Felicity had told Jane, this man Gabe was a shark: a great white, who ate up his own species as well as other fish, without thought or conscience for the devastation he left behind him. The fact that he had agreed to have dinner with them at all had, according to Felicity, been more than she had ever hoped for.

The man sounded like a first-class bastard to Jane, not a man anyone would particularly want to do business with. But the Warners didn't seem to have any choice in the matter!

'I'm really pleased for you, Felicity,' she told the other woman warmly. 'But shouldn't you be returning to your guests...?' And then Jane could begin the unenviable task of clearing away. She never left a home without first doing this; it was part of the service that none of the mess from her catering would be left for the client to clean up. Paula and Rosemary would leave as soon as they had served coffee, but Jane would be here until the end of the evening.

But she didn't mind that. She would work an eighteen-hour day, as she had done a lot at the beginning, as long as she was independent. Free...

'Heavens, yes.' Felicity giggled now at her own social gaffe. 'I was just so thrilled, I had to come and tell you. I'll talk to you again later.' She gave Jane's arm a grateful squeeze before hurrying back to rejoin her guests in the dining-room, leaving a trail of the aroma of her expensive perfume behind her.

Jane shook her head ruefully, turning her attention to the dessert dishes. Under other circumstances, she and Felicity might have become friends. As it was, no matter how friendly they might have become today, Jane knew she would leave here this evening and not see Felicity again until—or if—the other woman needed her professional services again.

She readily admitted that it was a strange life she had chosen for herself. Her refined speech and obvious education—an education that had included, thank goodness, a cordon bleu cookery course—set her apart from many people, and yet the fact that she was an employee of Felicity's, despite being the owner of the business, meant she didn't 'belong' in that set of people, either.

A strange life, yes, but it was one that gave her great satisfaction. Although occasionally it was a lonely life.

'—really is an absolute treasure,' Felicity could be heard gushing out in the hallway. 'I don't know why she doesn't open up her own restaurant; there's no doubting it would be all the rage.' Her voice became louder as she entered the kitchen. 'Jane, I've brought someone to meet you,' she announced happily, a thread of excitement underlying her voice. 'I think he's fallen in love with your cooking,' she added flirtatiously.

There was no warning. No sign. No alarm bells. Nothing to tell Jane that her life was about to be turned upside down for the second time in three years!

She picked up the towel to dry her hands before turning, fixing a smile on her lips as she did so, only to have that smile freeze into place as she looked at the man Felicity had brought into the kitchen to meet her.

No!

Not him!

It couldn't be!

She was successful. Independent. *Free.*

It couldn't be him. She couldn't bear it. Not when she had worked so hard.

'This is Gabriel Vaughan, Jane.' Felicity introduced him innocently. 'Gabe, our wonderful cook for the evening, Jane Smith.' She beamed at the two of them.

The Gabe Felicity had been chattering on about all afternoon had been Gabriel Vaughan? *The* Gabriel Vaughan?

Of course it was—he was standing across the kitchen from where Jane stood as if she had been turned to stone. He was older, of course—but then, so was she!—but the granite-like features of his face still looked as if they had been hewn from solid rock, despite the fact that he was smiling at her.

Smiling at her? It was the last thing he would be doing if he had recognised her in return!

'Jane Smith,' he greeted in a voice that perfectly matched the unyielding hardness of him.

He would be thirty-nine now. His dark hair was slightly overlong, easily brushing the collar of his dinner jacket, and he had a firmly set jaw, sculptured lips, a long, aristocratic nose jutting out arrogantly beneath the only redeeming feature in that hard face—eyes so blue they were almost aquamarine, like the clear, warm sea Jane had once swum in off the Bahamas, long, long ago.

'Or may I call you Jane?' he added charmingly, his American accent softening that harshness.

The black evening suit and snowy white shirt that Gabriel Vaughan wore with such disregard for their elegance did little to hide the power of the body beneath. His wide shoulders rippled with muscle; his height, at least six feet four inches, meant that he would easily tower over most men he would meet. At only five feet two inches tall herself, Jane had to bend her neck backwards to look up into that harshly carved face, a face that seemed to have become grimmer in the last few years, despite the fact that he was directing a charming smile in her direction at this moment.

Oh, Paul, Jane cried inwardly, how could you ever have thought to come up against this man and win?

But then, Paul hadn't won, had he? she acknowledged dully. No one ever had against Gabe, if the past newspaper reports about this man were to be believed. In fact, now that she knew who Felicity and Richard Warner were dealing with, she believed Felicity might be rather premature in her earlier feelings of celebration!

'Jane will be fine,' she answered him in the soft, calm voice she had learnt to use in every contingency over the last three years—although she was inwardly surprised she had managed to do so on this occasion!

This was Gabriel Vaughan she was talking to, the man who had ripped through the fabric of her life as if he were a tornado. She was damn sure he had never looked back to see what destruction he had left behind him!

'I'm pleased you enjoyed your meal, Mr Vaughan,' she added dismissively, hoping he would now return to the dining-room with his hostess. Outwardly she might appear calm, but her legs were already starting to shake, and it was only a matter of time before they would no longer support her!

He gave an inclination of his head, the overhead light making his dark hair almost appear black, although there were touches of grey now visible amongst that darkness. 'Your husband is a very lucky man,' he drawled softly.

Questioningly, it seemed to Jane. She resisted the impulse to glance down at her now bare left hand, knowing that not even an indentation now remained to show she had once worn a gold band there. 'I'm not married, Mr Vaughan,' she returned distantly.

He looked at her steadily for long, timeless seconds, taking in everything about her as he did so. And Jane was aware of everything he would see: nondescript brown hair restrained from her face with a black velvet band at her nape, pale, make-upless features dominated by huge brown eyes, her figure obviously slender, but her businesslike cream blouse and black skirt doing nothing to emphasise her shapeliness.

What Jane didn't see when she looked at her own reflection in the mirror—and would have been horrified if she had!—were the red highlights in the abundance of the shoulder-length hair she was at such pains to keep confined, or the stark contrast between that dark curling hair and the pale magnolia of her face, those huge brown eyes often taking on the same deep sherry colour of her hair. Her nose was small, her mouth having a sensual fullness she could do little to hide—despite not wearing lipgloss. In fact, she deliberately wore no make-up, but her face was peaches and cream anyway, adding to the hugeness of her captivating brown eyes. And, for all she believed her clothes to be businesslike, the cream blouse was a perfect foil for her colouring, and the knee-length of her skirt could do little to hide the curvaceousness of her long, silky legs.

'May I say,' Gabriel Vaughan murmured huskily, his bright blue gaze easily holding hers, 'that fact is to one poor man's detriment—and every other man's delight?'

'My dear Gabe,' Felicity teased, 'I do believe you're flirting with Jane.' She was obviously deeply amused by the fact.

He gave the other woman a mocking glance. 'My dear Felicity,' he drawled dryly, 'I do believe I am!' He turned back challengingly to Jane.

Flirting? With her? Impossible. If only he knew—

But he didn't know. He didn't recognise her. There was no way he would be looking at her with such warm admiration if he did!

Was she so changed? Facially, more mature, yes. But the main change, she readily accepted, was in her hair. Deliberately so. Once her hair had reached down to her waist, a straight curtain the golden colour of ripe corn— a stark contrast to the shoulder-length chestnut-brown it now was. She had been amazed herself at the difference the change of colour and style made to her whole appearance, seeming to change even the shape of her face. And eyes she had always believed were just brown had taken on the rich colour of her hair, the pale skin that was natural to her blonde hair becoming magnolia against the rich chestnut.

Yes, she had changed, and deliberately so, but until this moment, with Gabriel Vaughan looking at her with a complete lack of recognition, she hadn't realised just how successful she had been in effecting that change!

'Mr Vaughan...' She finally found her voice to answer him, her shocked surprise under control, if not eliminated. She was Jane Smith, personal chef to the beautiful and affluent, and this man was just another guest at one of those dinner parties she catered for. He shouldn't even be out here in the kitchen! 'I do believe—' she spoke slowly but firmly '—that you're wasting your time!'

His smile didn't waver for a second, but that brilliant blue gaze sharpened with interest. 'My dear Jane—' he lingered over the deliberate use of her first name, well aware of her own formality '—I make a point of never doing that.'

Outwardly she again remained calm, but inwardly she felt a shiver of apprehension down her spine. And it was a feeling she hadn't known for three years...

'Now, Gabe,' Felicity cut in laughingly, linking her arm through his, 'I can't have you upsetting Jane,' she scolded lightly. 'Let's go back to the dining-room and have a liqueur, and let's leave poor Jane in peace.' She slanted an apologetic smile towards Jane. 'I'm sure she would like to get home some time before morning. Come on, Gabe,' she encouraged firmly as he still made no effort to move. 'Or Richard will think we've run away together!'

Gabriel Vaughan didn't join in her throaty laughter. 'Richard need have no worries like that on my account. You're a beautiful woman, Felicity,' he added to take the sting out of his initial remark, 'but other men's wives have never held any appeal for me.'

Jane drew in a sharp breath, swallowing hard. Because she knew the reason 'other men's wives never held any appeal' for Gabriel Vaughan. Oh, yes, she knew only too well.

'I'm sure Richard will be pleased to hear that,' Jane dismissed with a calmness that had now become second nature to her. 'But Felicity is quite right; I do still have a lot to do. And your coffee will be going cold.' She turned to smile at Paula and Rosemary as they returned from serving coffee and liqueurs. Their timing couldn't have been more perfect!

She willed Gabriel Vaughan to leave the kitchen now, before her calm shattered and her legs collapsed beneath her.

She had believed she had succeeded in pushing the past to the back of her mind, but at this moment she had a vivid image of three years ago when her own photograph had appeared side by side with this man's for days on end in all the national newspapers.

She had wanted to run away and hide then, and to all intents and purposes she had done so. And although he wasn't aware of it—and she hoped he never would be— the man who had once haunted her every nightmare, waking as well as asleep, had finally caught up with her!

He was still watching her, that intent blue gaze un- wavering, despite the urgings of his hostess to return to the dining-room. His behaviour, Jane knew, was border- ing on rudeness, but, as she was also aware, he was very conscious of the fact that he had the upper hand here this evening. In the process of buying out Richard Warner's ailing company, backed up by the millions of pounds that was his own personal fortune, he had no reason to do any other than what he pleased. And at this particular moment he wanted to look at Jane...!

Finally—when Jane was on the point of wondering just how much longer she could withstand that stare!—he visibly relaxed, smiling that lazily charming smile, his eyes once more that brilliant shining aqua. 'It was a pleasure meeting you, Jane Smith,' he murmured huskily, holding out his hand to her in parting.

Paula and Rosemary, after one wide-eyed glance in her direction at finding their hostess and one of her guests in the kitchen chatting away to Jane, had busied themselves washing up the dessert dishes Jane hadn't been able to deal with because of the interruption. And Felicity was smiling happily, still filled with what she considered the success of the evening. Only Jane, it seemed, was aware that she viewed that hand being held out to her—a long, ringless hand, filled with strength—as if it were a viper about to strike!

'Thank you,' she returned coolly, not about to return the pleasantry. If there were any 'pleasure' attached to this meeting then it was definitely all on his side!

But she knew she had no choice but to shake the hand held out to her. Not to do so would be inexplicable. At least, to everyone else in the room. She knew exactly why she didn't want to touch this man—his hand or any other part of him. And if he knew, if he realised, he wouldn't be holding out that hand of friendship either!

His hand was cool and dry, his grip firm. Not that Jane gave him much chance to do the latter, her hand against his only fleetingly.

Those startling blue eyes narrowed once again, his

hand falling lightly to his side. 'Perhaps we'll meet again,' he said huskily.

'Perhaps,' she nodded noncommittally.

And perhaps they wouldn't! She had managed to get through three years without bumping into this man, and if she had her way it would be another three years—or longer!—before it happened again. And as Gabriel Vaughan spent most of his time in his native America, with only the occasional swim into English waters in his search for fresh prey, that shouldn't be too difficult to achieve!

'I should be in England for several months.' He seemed to read at least some of her thoughts, instantly squashing them. 'In fact,' he added softly, 'I've rented an apartment for three months; I can't stand the impersonality of hotels.'

Three months! They could be as long, or short, as he made them!

'I hope you enjoy your stay,' she returned dismissively, turning away now, no longer able to even look at him. She needed to sit down, her legs shaking very badly now. Why didn't he just go?

She moved to put the clean dessert dishes back on the pine dresser across the room, and by the time she turned back again, he had gone.

Jane swayed weakly on her feet, moving to sit heavily on one of the pine chairs that stood around the kitchen table. In reality, Gabriel Vaughan could only have been in the kitchen a matter of minutes—it just seemed much, much longer!

'Gosh, he was handsome, wasn't he?' Rosemary sighed longingly as she finished drying her hands, seeming unaware of Jane's distress.

Handsome? She supposed he was. She just had more reason to fear him—fear him realising who she was—than she had to find him attractive. Although it was obvious from Paula's appreciative grin that she too had found Gabriel Vaughan 'handsome'.

'Looks are only skin-deep,' Jane dismissed sharply, feeling her strength slowly returning. 'And underneath those trappings of civilisation—' there was no denying how dazzlingly attractive Gabriel Vaughan had looked in his dinner suit, or the charm of his manner '—Gabriel Vaughan is a piranha!'

Paula made a face at her vehemence. 'He seemed rather taken with you,' she said speculatively.

Jane gave a derisive smile. 'Men like him are not "taken" with the hired help! Now, it's time you two went off home to your husbands,' she added teasingly as she stood up. 'I can deal with what's left here.'

In fact, she was glad of the time alone once the two women had left for home. She could almost convince herself, as she pottered about the kitchen putting dishes away, that everything was once again back to normal, that the encounter with Gabriel Vaughan had never happened. Almost...

But there was absolutely no reason for their paths to cross again. Lightning really didn't strike twice in the same place, did it? Of course it didn't! Just as having Gabriel Vaughan enter her life once again wouldn't happen...

Everything was cleared away, the last guest having taken their leave, when Felicity came back into the kitchen half an hour later. And she looked so happy, so vastly different from the worried woman Jane had spent the afternoon with, that Jane didn't have the heart to tell her of her earlier misgivings about the evening having been quite the success Felicity obviously considered it had been. The other woman would no doubt find that out for herself soon enough. After Gabriel Vaughan's meeting with Richard, no doubt!

'I can't thank you enough, Jane.' She smiled, looking tired, the evening obviously having been more of a strain than it had earlier appeared. 'I don't know how I would have managed without you.'

'You would have been just fine,' Jane said with certainty; Richard Warner obviously had a treasure in his young wife.

'I'm not so sure.' The other woman grimaced. 'But tomorrow will tell if it was all worth it!'

It certainly would! And Jane really hoped this nice couple weren't in for a deep disappointment. Although, given what she knew of Gabriel Vaughan, it didn't auger well...

Felicity yawned tiredly. 'I think I'll go up to bed. Richard's just bringing through the last of the glasses. But leave them, Jane,' she insisted firmly. 'You must be much more tired than I am—and I'm staggering!' She walked to the kitchen door. 'Please go home, Jane,' she added with another yawn, turning before leaving the room. 'By the way, you made a definite hit this evening.' She raised auburn brows pointedly. 'Gabe was very interested.'

Jane forced herself to once again remain outwardly composed, revealing none of her inner panic. 'How interested?' she drawled lightly.

'Very.' Felicity smiled knowingly. 'I shouldn't be at all surprised if you and he meet again.'

She drew her breath in sharply. 'And what makes you think that?' she prompted tautly, still managing to keep a tight control over her nerves. Although it was becoming increasingly difficult to do so, the longer they discussed Gabriel Vaughan!

Surely he hadn't continued to be curious about her once he and Felicity had returned to the dinner party? There had been two other couples present, and Richard's recently divorced sister had been included to make up the eight; and Jane certainly didn't think any of them would have been interested in listening to a conversation about the caterer!

'Well, he— Ah, Richard,' Felicity moved aside so that her husband could enter the kitchen to put down the glasses. 'I was just telling Jane that I'm sure she and Gabe are going to meet again,' she said archly.

Richard shot an affectionate smile at his wife. He was in his early thirties, tall and blond, with young Robert Redford good looks, and had a perfect partner in his vivacious wife. 'Stop your matchmaking, darling. I'm sure Jane and Gabe are more than capable of making their own arrangements. If necessary,' he added with a rueful glance at Jane.

'It never hurts to give these things a helping hand.' Felicity gave another tired yawn.

'Will you please go to bed, Fliss?' her husband said firmly. 'I'll just see Jane out, and then I'll join you,' he promised.

And Jane wanted to leave; of that there was no doubt. But she had felt a chill inside her at Felicity's last statement. What had the other woman done to give a 'helping hand'?

'Okay,' Felicity concurred sleepily. 'And I do thank

you so much for doing this for us at such short notice, Jane. You've been wonderful!'

'My pleasure,' she dismissed lightly. 'But I can't help but feel curious as to why you should think Mr Vaughan and myself will meet again,' she persisted.

'Because he asked for your business card, darling,' the other woman supplied happily. 'He said it was so that he could call you when he gave his next dinner party, but I have a feeling you'll hear from him much sooner than that! Don't be too long, darling.' She smiled glowingly at her husband before finally going upstairs to their bedroom.

'I'm sorry about all that nonsense, Jane,' Richard said distractedly, running agitated fingers through the thickness of his blond hair. 'Fliss has been so worried these last few weeks, and that isn't good for her in early pregnancy. But take it from me: Gabe Vaughan is the last man you should become involved with,' he added grimly. 'He would gobble you up and spit you out again before you had a chance to say no!'

Gabriel Vaughan was the last man she ever *would* become involved with!

She had been frozen into immobility since Felicity's announcement of having given Gabriel Vaughan her business card, but she moved now, hurriedly putting on her jacket. 'I didn't realise Felicity was pregnant,' she said slowly. The other woman was so slim and elegant, the pregnancy certainly couldn't be very far along yet, and Felicity hadn't mentioned it. She had no doubt this happily married couple were pleased about the baby, but at the same time she realised it had probably happened at a bad time for them, what with the uncertainty about Richard's business.

'Only just.' Richard gave what looked like a strained smile. 'Felicity is longing to give me a son. Although at this rate there will be no business for him to grow up and take over!' he added bleakly. He shook his head self-derisively. 'Much as I also appreciate all that you've done this evening, Jane, unlike Felicity I think it's going to take a little more than an exceptional meal to convince Gabriel Vaughan that my company is worth saving rather than being gathered up into his vast, faceless business pool!'

Jane was inclined to agree with him. From what she knew of the ruthless American, he wasn't into 'saving' companies, only taking them over completely!

She certainly didn't envy Richard Warner his meeting with the older man tomorrow!

She reached out to squeeze his arm understandingly. 'I'll keep my fingers crossed for you,' she told him softly before straightening. 'Now I have to be on my way—and I think you should go upstairs and give your lovely wife a hug! There's a lot to be said for having a loyal wife and a beautiful family like you have, you know,' she added gently, having no doubts that Felicity would stand by her husband, no matter what the outcome of his meeting with Gabriel Vaughan.

Richard looked at her blankly for several seconds, and then he laughed softly. 'How right you are, Jane,' he agreed lightly. 'How right you are!'

She was well aware that it sometimes took someone outside the situation to remind one of how fortunate one was. And, no matter what happened tomorrow, this man would still have his beautiful wife and daughters, and their unborn child. And that was certainly a lot more than very many other people had.

And sometimes, Jane remembered bleakly as she left the house, all the positive things you thought you had in your life could be wiped out or simply taken away from you And a prime example of that had been this evening when Gabriel Vaughan had turned out to be the guest of honour at the Warners' dinner party! She had worked so hard to build up this business, to build something for herself—she would not allow it all to be wiped out a second time!

It had not been a good evening for Jane. First that broken cup—which she would replace, despite Felicity's protests that it wasn't necessary—then Gabriel Vaughan coming into the kitchen: the very last man she'd ever wanted to see again! Ever! And Felicity, poor romantic Felicity, had given him Jane's business card!

What else could possibly go wrong tonight?

She found that out a few minutes later—when her van wouldn't start!

CHAPTER THREE

JANE almost choked over her morning mug of coffee! As it was, her hand shook so badly that she spilt some of that coffee onto the newspaper that lay open on the break-fast-bar in front of her, the liquid splashing onto the smiling countenance of the man's face that had caused her to choke in the first place!

Gabriel Vaughan!

But then, nothing seemed to have gone right for her since meeting the man the evening before. It had been past one o'clock in the morning when she'd discovered her van wouldn't start, and a glance towards the Warners' house had shown her that it was in darkness. And, in the circumstances, Jane had been loath to disturb the already troubled couple. Besides, she had decided, if Richard Warner had any sense, he would be making love to his wife at this very moment—and she certainly had no inclination to interrupt that!

But it had been too late to contact a garage, and there had been no taxis cruising by in the exclusive suburb, and finding a public telephone to call for a taxi hadn't proved all that easy to do, either. And when she'd come to leave the call box after making the call it was to find it had begun to rain. Not gentle, barely discernible rain, but torrents of it, as if the sky itself had opened up and dropped the deluge.

Tired, wet and extremely disgruntled, she had finally arrived back at her apartment at almost two-thirty in the morning. And opening her newspapers at nine o'clock the following morning, and being confronted by a photograph of a smiling Gabriel Vaughan, was positively the last thing she needed!

This was the time of day when she allowed herself a few hours' relaxation. First she would go for her morning run, collecting her newspaper, and freshly baked croissants from her favourite patisserie on the way back. She had made a career out of cooking for other people, but she wasn't averse to sampling—and enjoying—other people's cooking in the privacy of her own home. And François's croissants, liberally spread with butter and honey, melted in the mouth.

But not this morning. She hadn't even got as far as taking her first mouthful, and now she had totally lost her appetite. And all because of Gabriel Vaughan!

She would never see him again, she had assured herself in the park earlier as her feet pounded on the pathway as she ran, slender in her running shorts and sweatshirt, her hair tied back with a black ribbon. As far as she was aware, the man had only paid brief visits to England over the last three years, and just because he had rented an apartment for three months that didn't mean he would actually stay that long. Once his business with Richard Warner had reached a suitable conclusion—to Gabriel Vaughan's benefit, of course!—he would no doubt be returning to America. And staying there, Jane hoped!

But this photograph in this morning's newspaper—of Gabriel with a dazzling blonde clinging to his arm—had been taken while at a weekend party given by a popular politician. It seemed to imply that his rare visits to this country in recent years had in no way affected his social popularity when he was here.

Jane stood up impatiently, her relaxation totally ruined for this morning. Damn the man! He had helped ruin her life once—she couldn't allow him to do it again, not when she had worked so hard to make a life and career for Jane Smith.

Jane Smith.

Yes, that was who she was now.

She drew in a deeply controlling breath, forcing back the panic and anger, bringing back the calm that had become such a necessary part of her for the last few years, reaching out as she did so to close the newspaper, not taking so much as another glance at the photograph that had so disturbed her minutes ago.

She had a job to do, another dinner party to arrange for this evening, and the first thing on her list of things to do was to check with the garage she had called earlier, and see if they had had any luck in starting her van. If it wasn't yet fixed she would have to hire alternative transport for the next few days.

Yes, she had a business to run, and she intended running it!

Despite Gabriel Vaughan.

Or in spite of him!

'Hell, I hate these damned things! If you're there, Jane Smith, pick up the damned receiver!'

Jane reached out with trembling fingers and switched off the recorded messages on her answer machine, quickly, as if the machine itself were capable of doing her harm. Which, of course, it wasn't. But the recorded message of that impatient male voice—even though the man hadn't given his name but had slammed the receiver down when he received no reply to his impatience—was easily recognisable as being that of Gabriel Vaughan.

She had telephoned the garage before taking her shower, had been informed that it would be ready for collection in half an hours' time, once they had replaced the old and worn battery. Then she'd showered quickly before switching on her answer machine as she usually did when she had to go out.

She had only been out of her apartment for an hour, but the flashing light on the answer machine had told her she had five messages. The first two had been innocuous enough—enquiries about bookings, which she would deal with before she went out to collect her supplies for this evening's dinner party. But the third call—! He didn't even need to say who it was—she could recognise that Transatlantic drawl anywhere!

It wasn't even twelve hours since she had left the Warners' home; the damned man had left no time at all before trying to contact her again!

What did he want?

Whatever it was, she wasn't interested. Not on a personal or professional level. On a personal level, he was the last man she wanted anything to do with, and the same applied on a professional level. For the same reason. The less contact she had with Gabriel Vaughan—on any level—the better she would like it.

That decision made, she decided to totally ignore the call, pretend it never happened. After all, he hadn't left a name or contact number, just those few words of angry impatience.

Having so decided, she reached out to switch the machine back on. After all, she had a business to run.

'Jane! Oh, Jane...!' There was a short pause in the fourth message, before the woman continued. 'It's Felicity Warner here. Give me a call as soon as you come in. Please!' Felicity had sounded tearful enough at the beginning of the message, but that last word sounded like a pleading sob!

And Jane didn't need two guesses as to why the other

woman had sounded so different on the recording from the happily excited one she had left the evening before; no doubt Richard had been to his meeting with Gabriel Vaughan!

Maybe she should have tried to warn the other woman last night, after all, once she had realised who Richard was dealing with? But if she had done that Felicity would only have wanted to know how she knew so much about the man. And it had taken her almost three years to shake off the how and why she had ever known a man like Gabriel Vaughan.

But Felicity sounded desperately upset, so unhappy. Which really couldn't be good for her in her condition—

'Don't you ever switch this damned thing off, Jane Smith?' The fifth message began to play, Gabriel Vaughan's voice sounding mockingly amused this time—and just as instantly recognisable to Jane as on the previous message. 'Well, I refuse to talk to a machine,' he continued dismissively. 'I'll try you again later.' He rang off abruptly, again without actually saying who the caller had been.

But Jane was in no doubt whatsoever who the caller had been, remembered all too well from last night when he had called her 'Jane Smith' in that mocking drawl. Two calls in a hour! What did the man want?

Some time in the last hour—if Felicity's cry for help was anything to go by—he had also spoken to Richard Warner!

The man was a machine. An automaton. He bought and sold, ruined people's lives, without a thought for the consequences. And the consequences, in this case, could be Felicity's pregnancy...!

Once again Jane switched off the answer machine. She didn't want to get involved in this, not from any angle.

And if she returned Felicity's call she would become involved. If she wasn't already!

She didn't really know the Warners that well. She understood they had been guests at several other dinner parties she had catered for, which was why Felicity had telephoned her for the booking last night.

Over the years Jane had made a point of not getting too close to clients; she was employed by them, and so she never, ever made the mistake of thinking she was anything else. But somehow yesterday had been different. Felicity had obviously been deeply worried, had desperately needed someone she could talk to. And she had chosen Jane as that confidante, probably because she realised, with the delicacy of Jane's position working in other people's homes, that she had to be discreet, that the things Felicity talked to her about would go no further.

Jane never had been a gossip, but now there was a very good reason why what Felicity had told her would go no further: she simply had no one she could possibly tell!

Her life was a busy one, and she met lots of people in the course of her work, but friends, good friends, were something she had necessarily moved away from in recent years. It was an unspoken part of her contract that she never discussed the people she worked for, and Jane guarded her own privacy even more jealously!

Her life had taken a dramatic turn three years ago, but determination and hard work meant she now ran her own life, and her own business. Successfully.

That success meant she could afford to rent this apartment; it was completely open-plan, with polished wood floors, scatter rugs, antique furniture, and no television, because not only did she not have the time to watch it, but she didn't like it either, her relaxation time spent listening to her extensive music collection, and reading the library of books that took up the whole of one wall. It was all completely, uniquely her own, and her idea of heaven on an evening off wasn't to go out partying as she would once have done, but to sit and listen to one of her favourite classical music tapes while rereading one of her many books.

But somehow those last three messages on her answer machine seemed even to have invaded the peace and tranquillity of her home...

Much as she liked Felicity and felt sorry for the other woman, she simply couldn't return that beseeching telephone call.

She just couldn't...!

She was tired by the time she returned to her apartment at one o'clock the following morning. The dinner party had been a success, but the reason for her weariness was the disturbance in her personal life over the last twenty-four hours.

The answer machine was flashing repeatedly—one, two, three, four, five, six, she counted warily. How many of those calls would be from Gabriel Vaughan?

Or was she becoming paranoid? The man she had met the evening before did not look as if he had to chase after any woman, least of all one who cooked for other people for a living! And yet on the second of those last recorded messages he had said he would 'try again later'!

Jane sighed. She was tired. It was late. And she wanted to go to bed. But would she be able to sleep, knowing that there were six messages on her machine that hadn't been listened to?

Probably not, she conceded with impatient anger. She

didn't like this. Not one little bit. She deeply resented Gabriel Vaughan's intrusion, but at the same time she was annoyed at her own reaction to it. She was not about to live in fear ever again. This was her home, damn it, her space, and Gabriel Vaughan was not welcome in it. He certainly wasn't going to invade it.

She reached out and firmly pushed the 'play' button on the answermachine.

'Hello, Jane, Richard Warner here. Felicity wanted me to call you. She's been taken into hospital. The doctor thinks she may lose the baby. I—she—Thank you for all your help last night.' The message came to an abrupt end, Richard Warner obviously not knowing what else to say.

Because there was nothing else to say, Jane realised numbly. What had Gabriel Vaughan said to Richard, what had he done, to have created such—?

No!

She couldn't become involved. She dared not risk—dared not risk—She just didn't dare!

But Felicity had called her earlier today, feeling that in some way she needed Jane. And, from Richard's call just now, the other woman had been proved right! Could Jane now just ignore this call for help? Or was it already too late...?

She couldn't change anything even if she did return Richard's call. What could she do? She would be the last person Gabriel Vaughan would listen to—even if she reversed her own decision about never wanting to speak to him again.

But what about Felicity...?

It was almost one-thirty in the morning now—too late to call either Richard or the hospital; she doubted the nurses on duty at the latter would volunteer any information about Felicity, anyway. She would go to bed, get a good night's sleep, and try calling Richard in the morning. Maybe Felicity's condition would be a little more positive by then.

Or maybe it wouldn't.

She absently listened to the rest of her messages, curious now about the other five calls.

They were all business calls, not a single one in the Transatlantic drawl she had quickly come to recognise—and dread—as being that of Gabriel Vaughan. And after those two calls this morning within an hour of each other his silence this evening did not reassure her. It unnerved her!

'She's—stable—that's how the doctor described her condition to me this morning,' Richard Warner told Jane in answer to her early morning telephone query about Felicity. 'Whatever that means,' he added disgustedly.

'What happened, Richard?' Jane prompted abruptly.

This call was against her better judgement; it came completely from the softness of emotions that she must never allow to rule her a second time. But she couldn't, she had decided in the clear light of day, simply ignore Felicity's and Richard's telephone calls.

'What do you think? Gabriel Vaughan is what happened!' Richard told her bitterly—and predictably!

Gabriel Vaughan seemed to just sail through life, sweeping away anything and anyone who should happen to stand in his way. And at the moment Richard Warner was in his way. Tomorrow, next week, next month, it would be someone else completely, any consequences that might follow Gabe's actions either ignored or simply unknown to him.

'I would really rather not talk about it, Jane,' Richard added agitatedly. 'At the moment my company is in chaos, my wife is in hospital—and just talking about Gabriel Vaughan makes my blood-pressure rise! I'll tell Felicity you rang,' he added wearily. 'And once again, thank you for all your help.' He rang off.

And a lot of good her help had done them, Jane sighed as she replaced her own receiver. Gabriel Vaughan had happened—who else…? What else? He was a man totally without—

Jane almost fell off her chair as the telephone beside her began to ring. Eight-fifteen. It was only eight-fifteen in the morning; she had deliberately telephoned Richard Warner this early so that she could speak to him before he either left for the office or the hospital. But she wasn't even dressed yet herself, let alone taken her run; who on earth—?

Suddenly she knew exactly who. And, after her recent calls from the Warners, and her conversation with Richard just now, she was in exactly the right frame of mind to talk to him!

She snatched up the receiver. 'Yes?' she snapped, all of her impatience evident in that single word.

'I didn't get you out of bed, did I, Jane Smith?' Gabriel Vaughan returned in his mocking drawl.

Her hand tightened about the receiver. She had known it was him—it couldn't have been anyone else, in the circumstances!—but even so she couldn't help her instant recoil just at the sound of his voice.

She drew in a steadying breath. 'No, Mr Vaughan,' she answered calmly, 'you didn't get me out of bed.' And, remembering what she had once been told about this man, she knew that he had probably already been up for hours, that he only needed three or four hours' sleep a night.

'I didn't—interrupt anything, did I?' he continued derisively.

'Only my first coffee of the morning,' she bit out tersely.

'How do you take it?'

'My coffee?' she returned, frowning.

'Your coffee,' he confirmed, laughter evident in his voice now.

'Black, no sugar,' she came back tautly—and then wished she hadn't. In retrospect, she could think of only one reason why he would be interested in how she liked her first cup of coffee of the morning!

'I'll make sure I remember that,' Gabriel Vaughan assured her huskily.

'I'm sure you didn't call me to find out how I take my coffee,' Jane snapped, sure that he remembered most things.

Except that other her, it seemed But how long would that last? Three years on, and not only did she look different, she *was* different, but Gabriel Vaughan had a very good reason for remembering everything that had happened three years ago, leading her to believe that his memory lapse where she was concerned would not continue. She had no doubt there would be no flirtatious early morning telephone calls then!

'You're wrong there, Jane Smith,' he murmured throatily now. 'You see, I want to know everything about you that there is to know—including how you take your coffee!'

Jane's breath left her in a shaky sigh, her hand tightening painfully about the receiver. 'I'm an extremely boring individual, I can assure you, Mr Vaughan,' she told him abruptly.

'Gabe,' he put in smoothly. 'And I very much doubt *that*, Jane,' he added teasingly.

She didn't care what he doubted. She worked, she went to bed, she ran, she shopped, she read, she worked, she went to bed Her life was structured, deliberately so. Routine, safe, uncomplicated. This man threatened complications she didn't even want to think about!

'Are you aware that Felicity Warner is in hospital, in danger of losing her baby?' she attacked accusingly.

There was a slight pause on the other end of the telephone line. Very short, only a second or two, but Jane picked up on it anyway. To her surprise. Three years ago nothing had deterred this man. And she couldn't really believe that had changed in any way.

'I wasn't aware that Felicity was pregnant,' he finally rasped harshly.

'Would it have made any difference if you had known?' Jane scorned disgustedly, already knowing the answer to that question. Nothing distracted this man away from his purpose. And she couldn't help feeling that he had been playing with the Warners by accepting their dinner invitation two evenings ago...!

'Any difference to what?' he returned in a silkily soft voice.

'Let's not play games, Mr Vaughan.' She continued to be deliberately formal, despite his earlier invitation for her not to be. 'You have business with Richard Warner, and that business appears to be affecting his wife's health. And that of their unborn child,' she added shakily. 'Don't you think—?'

'I'm not sure you would like to hear what I think, Jane Smith,' Gabriel Vaughan bit out coldly.

'You're right—I don't,' she snapped tersely. 'But I think it's way past time someone told you about your lack of thought for the people lives you walk into and instantly dismantle! Your method of dealing with people leaves a lot to be desired, and—' She broke off abruptly, feeling the icy silence at the other end of the telephone line as it blasted its way in her direction. And at the same time she realised she had said too much...

'And just what do you know about my "method of dealing with people", Jane Smith?' he prompted mildly—too mildly for comfort!

Too much. She had said too much! 'You're a public figure, Mr Vaughan.' She attempted to cover up her lapse.

'Not in England,' he rasped. 'Not for several years,' he added harshly, all his previous lazy charm obliterated in cold anger.

'Strange; I'm sure I saw your photograph in my daily newspaper yesterday morning...' she came back pointedly; she had to try and salvage this conversation as best she could; she'd already been far too outspoken.

The last thing she wanted to do was increase this man's interest in her! Ideally, she would like him to forget he had ever met someone called Jane Smith, but she would settle for disinterest—which wasn't going to be achieved if she kept challenging him!

'Of course, that was a social thing,' she added lightly. 'You were a guest at a party.'

'I'm a sociable person, Jane,' he drawled dryly. 'Which was actually the reason for this call...'

He was going to ask her to cater a dinner party for him! There was no way she could work for or with this man. Absolutely no way!

'I'm very heavily booked at this time of year, Mr Vaughan,' she told him stiffly: Christmas was now only two weeks away. 'My diary has been full for weeks, some of those bookings made months ago. However, I could recommend another catering firm who I'm sure would be only too pleased to—'

Gabriel Vaughan's husky laugh cut in on her businesslike refusal. 'You misunderstood me, Jane,' he murmured, that laugh still evident in his voice. 'I was asking you to have dinner with me, not trying to book your services as a cook—impressive as they might be!'

Now it was Jane's turn to fall silent. Not because she was angry, as Gabriel Vaughan had been minutes ago—where had that anger gone...? No, she was stunned. Gabriel Vaughan was asking her for a date. Impossible. He just didn't realise how impossible that was.

'No,' she said abruptly.

'Just—no?' he said slowly, musingly. 'You don't even want a little time to think about it?'

She doubted too many women had to do that where this man was concerned; he was handsome, single, undoubtedly rich, sophisticated, witty—what more could any woman want?

All Jane knew was that she did not want Gabriel Vaughan!

'No,' she repeated sharply.

'Then I take it I was right earlier in assuming there's someone else in your life,' he dismissed hardly, a chill edging his tone.

Jane frowned. When earlier in this conversation had he assumed there was already someone else in her life? They hadn't even touched on the subject.

'I have no idea what you're talking about,' she snapped.

'It's occurred to me, Jane, that you have an unhealthy interest—as far as Felicity goes—in Richard Warner's affairs. And I don't just mean his business ones!' he added harshly.

'You're disgusting, Mr Vaughan,' Jane told him angrily. 'Other women's husbands have never held any appeal for me, either!' She deliberately threw his words to Felicity two evenings ago back in his face, then slammed down the receiver, immediately switching on the answer machine.

She didn't think Gabriel Vaughan was the sort of man to ring a woman back when she had angrily terminated their telephone conversation, but on the off chance that he just might she had no intention of answering that call herself.

He had just implied she was having an affair with Richard Warner!

How dared he?

CHAPTER FOUR

'WE MEET again, my dear Jane Smith.'

Jane froze in the act of placing the freshly baked meringues onto the cooling tray, closing her eyes briefly, hoping this was only a nightmare. One that she would wake up from at any second!

But closing her eyes achieved nothing, because she could smell his aftershave now, and knew that when she turned Gabriel Vaughan was going to be standing only feet behind her. Could it only be coincidence that this was the second dinner party in a week that she had catered for where Gabriel Vaughan was a guest...?

She opened her eyes, straightening her shoulders before turning sharply to face him, her heart missing a beat as the total masculinity of him suddenly dominated the kitchen in which she had worked so harmoniously for the last four hours.

She was realising that he was a man who wore a black evening suit and white shirt with a nonchalance that totally belied the exclusive cut of the expensive material. He was vibrantly attractive, in a way that stated he didn't give a damn how he looked, that he was totally confident of his own masculinity, the challenging glitter of those aqua-blue eyes daring anyone to question it.

To her dismay, Jane realised that was probably exactly what she had done two days ago when she had turned down his invitation to dinner!

She gave a cool inclination of her head. 'You mentioned that you're a sociable person,' she dismissed coldly.

'And you,' Gabe returned mockingly, 'mentioned how busy you were for the next few weeks.' He shrugged. 'The mountain came to Mohammed!'

Her eyes narrowed warily. Could this man possibly have—? No, she couldn't believe he would go to the extreme of having himself invited to a dinner party she was catering simply so that he— Couldn't she...? Hadn't the hostess this evening telephoned her earlier this morning and apologetically explained that, if it wasn't going to be too much of a problem for her, there would be two extra guests for dinner this evening. Was Gabriel Vaughan one of those guests...?

'I see,' she murmured noncommittally. 'I hope you're enjoying the meal, Mr Vaughan,' she added dismissively.

But Gabe wasn't to be dismissed, leaning back against one of the kitchen units, totally relaxed—at least, on the surface; he must have been as aware as she was that the last time the two of them had spoken she had slammed the telephone down on him!

'I am now,' he assured her huskily, looking at her admiringly. 'That's quite a temper you have there, Jane Smith.' There was an edge of admiration in his mocking tone as he too recalled the abrupt end of their telephone conversation two days ago.

Jane returned his gaze unblinkingly. 'That was quite an accusation you made—Gabriel Vaughan,' she returned, undaunted.

He smiled. More of a grin really, deep grooves beside his mouth, teeth white against his tanned skin. 'Richard wasn't too happy about it, either,' he murmured with amusement.

Her eyes widened, the colour of rich sherry. 'You repeated that—that ridiculous accusation to him?' she gasped disbelievingly.

'Mmm,' Gabe acknowledged ruefully, his gaze lightly mocking. 'Tell me,' he continued consideringly, 'what *do* you do for exercise?'

She shook her head, totally amazed at this man's insulting conversation; he didn't even try to be polite!

'I run, Mr Vaughan,' she snapped angrily. 'And I really can't believe you were so insensitive as to have repeated such an accusation to Richard, at a time like this—'

'Felicity is out of hospital, you know.' Gabe straightened, not as relaxed as he had been; in fact he looked slightly defensive, the challenging look back in his eyes.

As it happened, Jane did know—but she was surprised he did. She hadn't actually gone in to see Felicity when she was in hospital, but she had telephoned the hospital to pass on her well wishes, and she had called Richard every day to check on his wife's condition, relieved when she'd spoken to him this morning and heard that the doctor considered Felicity well enough to go home, the miscarriage in abeyance. For the moment. But surely if this man continued his hounding of Richard—and throwing out obscene accusations—that may not last...!

'How long for?' Jane scorned. 'When do you intend making your next assault on Richard's company?' she added disgustedly.

'I don't assault, Jane,' Gabe drawled derisively. 'I acquire companies—'

'By going for the jugular of the owner!' she accused heatedly. 'Look for the weakness, and then go for it!'

Gabe looked completely unmoved by her accusation. But those aqua-blue eyes had narrowed and a pulse was beating in his clenched jaw. Maybe he wasn't as completely lacking in compassion as she had believed...

No, she couldn't believe that. Three years ago he had been completely ruthless, totally without compassion. It had been his behaviour then that had turned an unbearable situation into a living hell. It was the very reason she had reacted so strongly to Felicity and Richard's situation. For all the good that had done her—Gabriel Vaughan had taken her emotional response and immediately jumped to the conclusion that she must be having an affair with Richard!

'Every company has its weak spot, Jane,' Gabe mocked now. 'But I only acquire the ones that are of interest to me.' He pursed his lips thoughtfully. 'I don't wish to alarm you, Jane, but there appears to be smoke coming from—'

Her second batch of meringues!

Ruined. Burned, she discovered as she quickly opened the oven door and black smoke belched out into the kitchen.

'Don't be a fool!' Gabe rasped harshly, pushing her none too gently out of the way as she would have pulled the tray from inside the oven. 'You open the kitchen door, and I'll throw the tray out into the garden.' He took the oven-glove from her unresisting fingers. 'The door, Jane,' he prompted again firmly as she still didn't move.

Damn the man, she muttered to herself as she finally went to open the door. She couldn't remember the last time she had burnt anything, let alone in the middle of a dinner party. But this man had disturbed her so badly that he had achieved it quite easily. She was losing it, damn it. Damn him!

'Out of my way, Jane,' Gabe instructed grimly, going past her to throw the blackened meringues, and the tray, out into the garden.

Jane watched wordlessly as the burnt mess landed outside in the snow. Yes, snow. Somewhere, in the midst of
what was turning out to be a terrible evening—the second
in a week—it had begun to snow, a layer of white already
dusting everything, the overheated tray sizzling and
crackling in the coldness.

'Where do you run?'

She turned back to look at Gabriel Vaughan, dismayed
at how close he was to her as they both stood in the open
doorway, blinking up at him dazedly, the coldness of
their breath intertwining. 'The park near my apartment.
Why?' She frowned her sudden suspicion at the question.

His gaze remained unblinkingly on her own. 'Just curious.'

She shook her head, outwardly unmoved by his closeness, but inwardly…! But if she moved away he would
merely realise how disturbing she found it to be standing
this close to him. And as far as she was concerned he
already had enough of an advantage—even if he wasn't
aware of it!

And he could keep his damned curiosity to himself!
Not that it really mattered; he had no idea where she
lived, and so consequently he wouldn't know which park
it was, either!

'By the look of this snow—' she looked up into a sky
that seemed full of the heavy whiteness '—I won't be
running anywhere tomorrow morning.' Her morning run
in the nearby park cleared her head and set the tone for
the rest of her day, and finding Gabriel Vaughan there,
accidentally or otherwise, would totally nullify the exercise!

'A fair-weather runner, hmm?' Gabe drawled derisively.

Her brows rose indignantly over wide sherry-brown eyes. 'I don't—'

'Ah, Gabriel, this is where you've been hiding yourself,' murmured a husky female voice. 'What on earth is that dreadful smell?' Celia Barnaby, the hostess of the evening, a tall, elegant blonde, wrinkled her nose at the smell of the burnt meringues that still lingered in the kitchen.

Gabe looked down at Jane, winking conspiratorially before turning to stroll across the kitchen to join his hostess. 'I believe it was dessert, Celia,' he drawled laughingly, taking a light hold of her arm as he guided her back out of the kitchen. 'I think we should leave Jane alone so that she can do her best to salvage it in peace!'

'But—'

'I believe you were going to tell me about the skiing holiday you're taking in the New Year?' Gabe prompted lightly, continuing to steer the obviously reluctant Celia away from the disaster area. 'Aspen, wasn't it?' He glanced back at Jane over the top of the other woman's head, his smile one of intimate collusion.

'Damn the man,' Jane muttered to herself as she set about 'salvaging'; and she didn't have a lot of time to do it. Her two helpers for the evening were now returning with the empty vegetable dishes, as the main course had just been served.

By the time she had finished arranging the meringues and fruit on the plates, lightly covering the latter with a raspberry sauce, no one would ever have guessed that there should actually have been two meringues on each plate.

Except Gabriel Vaughan, of course. But then, he was the reason for the omission; if she hadn't been busy fending off his questions then this disaster wouldn't have happened. She was just too professional, too organised, for to this happen under normal circumstances. But with Gabriel Vaughan once again present it was far from normal!

In fact, she was slightly on edge for the rest of the evening, kept half expecting Gabriel Vaughan to stroll back into the kitchen unannounced; it just didn't seem to occur to him that the dinner guests weren't supposed to just stroll about the homes of their host or hostess, let alone go into the kitchen and chat to the hired help! That was his inborn arrogance, Jane decided derisively; Gabriel Vaughan would go where he wanted, when he wanted.

And he would also say exactly what he pleased, even if it was insulting!

She couldn't even imagine what Richard Warner must be thinking about the other man's accusations concerning the two of them. It was so ludicrous it would be laughable in other circumstances. As it was, she could imagine that Gabe's words that Richard 'wasn't too happy' about it were definitely an understatement where Richard was concerned!

It was extremely late by the time she had tidied away the last of the dishes from the meal, and she had to admit she was exhausted. But not from physical work; it was due entirely to tension. Unfortunately, she didn't manage to make her escape before Celia Barnaby came through to the kitchen, the last of her guests having finally left.

And it was unfortunate, because Celia wasn't one of Jane's favourite people. She was a beautiful divorcee, who had obviously only married her weak husband for the millions she had been able to take off him as part of their divorce settlement. Jane found her brittle and condescending, altogether too jaded.

Nevertheless she smiled politely at the other woman; she didn't have to like the people she worked for; it certainly wasn't conditional to her supplying the superb food she was known for. If that condition had applied two years ago, when she'd first begun this exclusive service, then she would have been out of work within a month!

Celia arched shaped brows. 'Have you and Gabriel known each other long?' she enquired lightly.

Jane gave her a startled look. This woman certainly didn't believe in the 'lead up to' approach! 'Known each other long...?' she repeated dazedly. The two of them didn't know each other at all!

'Mmm,' Celia drawled. 'Gabriel explained to me that the two of you are old friends.'

'He—!' Jane broke off, swallowing hard. 'He said that?' She frowned darkly.

'Don't be so coy, Jane.' The other woman gave her a knowing smile. 'I always thought you were a bit of a dark horse, anyway. And I've never understood why you became a brunette; did no one ever tell you blondes have more fun?' she drawled suggestively, looking disparagingly at Jane's hair.

Jane was totally stunned. By all that this woman had just said. For one thing, she was surprised this woman had ever spared her a second thought. And she was rendered speechless by that comment about blondes.

The change of colour and style to her hair, she had felt two and a half years ago, had been an important part of the new her. It wasn't only Gabriel Vaughan she didn't want recognising her; it wouldn't do for any of the people she worked for to realise she had once led a similar lifestyle to their own, either, and so the change in her appearance had served a double purpose. Until this moment she had thought the disguise worked, always took care to have her hair coloured once a month. Before now no one had ever told her they knew she was really a blonde!

On top of that Gabriel Vaughan's claim that the two of them were 'old friends' was just too much. Almost a week's acquaintance did not make them old friends—and she wouldn't term them as friends anyway!

Unless Gabriel Vaughan did remember her from three years ago, after all, and he was just playing with her...?

'Not very long, no.' She woodenly answered Celia's original question.

'Pity.' Celia grimaced her disappointment at her answer. 'I wondered what his wife had been like. You did know he's been married, didn't you?' She looked at Jane fron beneath lowered lashes.

Oh, yes, she knew he had been married, Jane acknowledged with an inward shiver. The death of Gabriel Vaughan's wife had only added to the spiralling out of control of her own life!

'Yes,' Jane confirmed abruptly. 'And surely you saw her photograph in the newspapers at the time of the accident?' She seemed to be having trouble articulating; her lips felt stiff and unmoving. It was so long since anyone had talked about these things...!

'Didn't everyone? Such a scandal, my dear,' Celia said with obvious relish. 'Jennifer Vaughan was so beautiful it made every other woman want to weep!' she added disgustedly. 'No, I know what she looked like, Jane; I just wondered what she was really like. I never actually met her, you see; I didn't know Gabriel in those days.'

Jane had never met Jennifer Vaughan either. But she had come to fear her, and the effect of her beauty.

'I can't be of any help to you there, I'm afraid, Celia,' she dismissed coolly, wanting to make good her escape now, and it had little to do with the lateness of the hour. All this talk of Jennifer Vaughan; it was unnerving! 'I've only met Gabriel since the death of his wife, too.' She was deliberately economical with the facts.

For herself she didn't care if Celia knew she and Gabriel Vaughan had only spoken for the first time a few days ago, but to tell the other woman that, in the face of Gabe's contradictory claim, would only arouse the other woman's curiosity even more. And that she didn't want!

'Oh, well.' Celia straightened, obviously realising she wasn't going to get much information out of Jane. 'It was a marvellous meal this evening, Jane,' she added off-handedly. 'You'll send your bill through, as usual?'

'Of course,' she nodded, and, as usual, Celia would delay paying it for as long as possible; for a woman with millions, she was very loath to pay her bills.

In fact, Jane had thought long and hard before agreeing to cater this dinner party. Celia could be extremely difficult to work for, and with the added problem of her reluctance to pay...

In view of the fact that Gabriel Vaughan had turned out to be one of the guests, she wished she had followed her instincts and said no, Jane told herself as she left the house, a blast of icy snow hitting her in the face. It was—

'Here, let me take that for you.' The box of personal utensils was plucked out of her hands, Gabriel Vaughan grinning at her unconcernedly over the top of it. 'Hurry up, Jane,' he encouraged as she stood rooted to the spot, stunned into immobility by his presence. 'It's still snowing!' he pointed out dryly, his mouth twisting derisively as he stated the obvious.

In actual fact, it was snowing heavier than ever, everywhere covered with it now, although luckily the roads looked to be clear. But it wasn't the snow or the conditions of the road that bothered her. What was Gabriel Vaughan still doing here? she'd thought he'd left some time ago.

She hoped Celia, inside the brightly lit house, didn't see the two of them outside together! Although, having spoken to Jane, and realising how little she actually knew about Gabriel Vaughan, the other woman had seemed to lose interest. Jane just hoped that Celia hadn't questioned Gabe in the way she had her—or mentioned the curious fact of Jane's dyed hair!

'Come on, Jane,' he urged impatiently, both of them having snowflakes in their hair now. 'Open up your van, where it's at least dry!'

She moved automatically to unlock the door and climbed inside, only to turn and find Gabe sitting in the passenger seat beside her. And looking very pleased with himself, too, his smile one of satisfaction now.

'What are you doing here?' Jane snapped irritably; she really had had enough for one night.

His mouth twisted derisively. 'That's a pretty blunt question, Jane,' he drawled.

'I'm a pretty blunt person—Mr Vaughan,' she bit out caustically. 'You see, I thought we had said all we have to say to each other earlier.'

He leant his head back against the seat as he gave her a considering look. The snow had melted on his hair, making it look darker than ever in the light blazing out from the house. 'What have I ever done to you, Jane, to provoke such animosity? Oh, I'll accept you don't like my business practices,' he continued unhurriedly before she could make a reply. 'But you said yourself—and Richard confirmed it—that you aren't involved with him, and Felicity didn't give me the impression the two of you are big buddies either, so what is the problem you have concerning my business dealings with Richard? You don't give the impression of someone who takes up a campaign against injustice on someone else's part—in fact, just the opposite!' He looked at her through narrowed lids.

Jane stiffened at this last statement. 'Meaning?' she prompted tautly.

He shrugged. 'Meaning you don't seem to me to be a person that likes to draw attention to yourself. That, like me, you prefer to shun the limelight.'

Her mouth twisted at the latter description. 'That sounds a little odd coming from someone whose photograph recently appeared in the daily newspapers!' There had been yet another mention of him yesterday after he'd attended a charity dinner. Thankfully, she hadn't reacted to it in the way she had the other morning, and she had managed not to spill any of her coffee, either! 'But then, you did mention that you're a sociable person!' she added mockingly.

Again he gave her that considering look, very still as he sat beside her. 'Believe it or not, Jane, I hate parties,' he finally drawled. 'And dinner parties are even more boring; whoever your dinner companion for the evening turns out to be, you're stuck with them! And this evening I was stuck between Celia and a woman old enough to be my grandmother!'

In fact, Jane knew, the elderly lady he was referring to was actually Celia's grandmother, a titled lady that Celia considered of social value. But as she was aged in her seventies, and slightly deaf, it was only too easy to guess why Celia had seated Gabe as she had; given the choice between talking to an elderly, slightly deaf lady and the beautiful Celia, Gabe would be sure to spend the

majority of the evening talking to Celia herself. Except
for those ten minutes or so when Gabe had joined Jane
in the kitchen.

'You hide your aversion to dinner parties very well,'
Jane told him dryly.

'You know exactly why I was at Richard and Felicity's
that evening,' Gabe rasped. 'Would you like to hear why
I was here tonight?' He quirked dark brows challengingly.

She looked at him, recognising that challenge, and suddenly she knew, in view of Celia's call this morning concerning two extra guests, that Gabe's reason for being
here tonight was the last thing she wanted to hear!

'It's late, Mr Vaughan.' She straightened in her seat,
putting the key in the ignition in preparation for leaving.
'And I would very much like to go home now,' she added
pointedly.

Gabe nodded. 'And exactly where is home?' he
prompted softly.

She glanced at him sharply. 'London, of course,' she
answered warily.

Gabe's mouth twisted wryly. 'It's a big place,' he
drawled. 'Close to one of the parks, I imagine— Your
running, Jane,' he explained at her sharp look. 'But
couldn't you be a little more specific?' he coaxed softly.

No, she couldn't; her privacy was something she
guarded with the ferocity of a lioness over her den! And
her apartment was her final point of refuge.

'You're a very difficult woman to pin down, Jane
Smith,' he murmured at her continued silence. 'No one
I've spoken to about you seems to have any idea where
you live. Clients contact you by telephone, bills are paid
to a post office box number, there's none of the usual
advertising on the side of your van—in fact, it's un-

marked.' He shook his head. 'Why all the secrecy, Jane?'

Jane stared at him with wide sherry-coloured eyes. He had talked to people about her? Tried to find out where she lived? Why?

'Why?' he repeated questioningly—making her aware that she had spoken the word out loud. 'Do you have any idea how beautiful you are, Jane Smith?' he asked her huskily, suddenly much closer in the confines of the van. 'And your damned elusiveness only makes you all the more intriguing!' He was so close now, the warmth of his breath stirred the wispy strands of her fringe.

She couldn't move, was held mesmerised by the intensity of those aqua-blue eyes, was transfixed by the sudden intimacy that had sprung up between them.

'Jane—'

'I don't think so, Mr Vaughan.' She flinched away from the caressing hand he laid against the nerve pulsing in her throat, straightening again in her seat, moving away from him as she did so. 'Now, would you please get out of my van?' she said angrily—not sure if that anger was directed at him or herself.

Had she really almost felt tempted to let him kiss her, as his warm gaze had promised he wanted to do as he'd moved closer to her? That would have been madness. Not only for her personally, but it would have threatened every vestige of peace she had built for herself over the last two years.

Gabe didn't move, frowning across at her. 'Was I wrong, and you are involved with someone? Is that why you protect your privacy so fiercely?' he rasped.

And why she flinched away from letting him kiss her? He didn't say the words, but the question was there anyway. Jane realised that, to him, a man used to getting what he wanted, and having any woman he wanted, her aversion to him had to have some explanation. Whereas the real reason for her aversion to him would probably send him into shock—before another emotion entirely took over!

'No,' she assured him dryly.

Blue eyes narrowed. 'No man,' he mused. 'How about a woman?' he added as if the thought had just occurred to him.

Jane gave a slight laugh. 'Or woman,' she added, with a derisive shake of her head.

He shrugged. 'You never can tell.' He excused his own grasping at straws. 'Look, Jane, I've been completely open with you from the first. I like you. I was drawn to you from the moment—'

'Please don't go on,' she cut in coldly. 'You're only going to embarrass me—as well as yourself!'

Anger flashed briefly across his face, his jaw hardening, and then he had himself under control again, relaxing as he smiled that slow, charming smile. 'I'm rarely embarrassed, Jane. And you don't get anywhere without asking,' he added huskily.

She shot him a chilling look. 'Most men would be gracious enough to accept what is definitely no for an answer!'

'Most men,' Gabe nodded. 'But I've invariably found that it's the things worth persisting for that are worth having,' he teased lightly, before glancing out of the van window. 'The snow appears to be getting heavier, so perhaps you should be getting home.' He reached for the door handle. 'Take care driving home, won't you?' came his parting shot.

She always took care, in everything that she did. And one of the biggest things she had taken care over was avoiding any possibility of meeting this man over the last three years. But now what she had always dreaded had happened; he had found her. And, for some inexplicable reason, he believed he was attracted to her!

He had tried to find her three years ago. He had pursued her until she had felt she couldn't run any longer, when the only answer had seemed to be to shake off all that she was, all that she had been. And with those changes—her name, her appearance—she had finally been able to make the life for herself that she had been searching for. How ironic, after all that had happened, that she should have Gabriel Vaughan to thank for making that possible!

But how long would it be, Jane wondered with a sinking heart as she drove home through the treacherous snow conditions, before Gabe saw through what was, after all, only a superficial disguise, and that attraction he believed he felt towards her turned into something much more ugly...?

CHAPTER FIVE

'I HAVE no idea what you said to him, Jane,' Felicity announced happily, 'but whatever it was I thank you for it!'

Jane had called in to see Felicity two days after Celia Barnaby's dinner party, having no bookings for that day and, having decided long ago that, no matter how good it was for business to have so many bookings in the run up to Christmas, she also needed a certain amount of time off. It would do business absolutely no good whatsoever if she should collapse under the strain.

There were plenty of other things she could have done with her day off, but she was very conscious of the fact that she hadn't actually visited the other woman since her discharge from hospital, and so she had called in after lunch.

But she couldn't actually say she liked the turn the conversation had taken once the two women were sitting down with a cup of tea. 'I'm sorry, Felicity.' She shook her head. 'I have no idea what you're talking about.' She gave a vaguely dismissive smile, appearing outwardly puzzled—she hoped. Inwardly she had an idea she knew exactly who 'him' was, even if she wasn't too sure what Gabriel Vaughan had done now. The one thing she was absolutely sure of was that whatever it was, she didn't come into it!

Felicity gave her a teasing smile, still taking things easy after the scare earlier in the week, although she certainly looked glowing enough this afternoon. 'From what

Richard told me,' Felicity grinned, 'I got the impression you had told Gabe exactly what you thought of him!'

Jane could feel the warm colour in her cheeks. 'Only from a business point of view,' she confirmed reluctantly.

Felicity raised auburn brows. 'Is there another point of view?'

'Not as far as I'm concerned, no,' Jane told the other woman flatly.

'Whatever,' Felicity accepted, giving Jane's arm an understanding squeeze. 'I'm not going to pry,' she assured her huskily. 'All I know is that instead of buying Richard out, and basically taking over the company, Gabe has agreed to financially back Richard until the company is back on its feet again.'

'Why?' Jane frowned; it sounded too good to be true to her. There had to be something in it for Gabriel Vaughan.

'Richard asked him the same question.' The other woman nodded knowingly. 'And do you know what his answer was?'

She couldn't even begin to guess. Didn't really want to know. But she had a feeling Felicity was going to tell her anyway!

'I have no idea,' she shrugged.

The other woman smiled. 'Gabe said it was because of something someone had said to him. And the only "someone" we could think of was you!'

Jane didn't believe that anything she could have said to Gabriel Vaughan could possibly have made any difference to his sudden change of plans where Richard's company was concerned. There had to be another reason for it. Although she very much doubted Gabe would decide to let any of them in on what it actually was. Until he was ready to, of course!

'I don't think so, Felicity,' she said dryly. 'Although I'm glad, for both your sakes, that he's decided to back off.' And she sincerely hoped, for Felicity's sake, that he didn't as quickly change his mind back again! 'But if I were Richard I would make the agreement legally binding as soon as possible,' she added derisively.

'Already done,' the other woman assured her happily. 'Gabe has his own legal team, and between them and Richard's lawyer they tied the deal up very neatly yesterday afternoon. I can't tell you how much better I feel, Jane.' Felicity sighed contentedly.

Jane could see how much more relaxed the other woman was; she just wished she felt the same way!

Unfortunately she didn't. As she drove back to her own apartment she was filled with disquieting feelings. Why had Gabriel Vaughan, when he had seemed so set on taking over Richard Warner's company, suddenly done an about face and come to a much less aggressive agreement with the other man?

Jane refused point-blank to believe it had anything to do with what she had said to him! The man was simply too hardened, too ruthless to be swayed by such things as human frailty in Felicity's case, and emotional accusations in hers. She should know!

So it wasn't the best time in the world, with her thoughts confused and worried, for her to arrive back outside her apartment, her arms full of the food shopping she had done on the way home, to find a huge bouquet of flowers lying outside her apartment front door!

For one thing the flowers, whoever they were from— and she had an uneasy feeling she knew exactly who that might be!—were completely unwelcome. She had made a decision, after the pain and disillusionment she had suffered three years ago, that no man, apparently nice or otherwise, would ever get close enough to her again to cause the complete destruction of her life that she had known then.

For a second thing, how had the flowers got all the way up here to her apartment in the first place? This was supposed to be a secure building, and her apartment on the fourth floor—laughingly called the penthouse apartment—could only be reached by the lift and fire-stairs. In which case, any flowers that had been delivered to the building should have been left downstairs in the vestibule between the outside door and the security door, a door that could only be unlocked by one of the four residents.

So just how had this bouquet of flowers arrived up here outside her door...?

'The lady in apartment number three let me in.' Gabriel Vaughan rose to his feet from the shadows of the hallway where he had obviously been sitting on the carpeted floor, walking slowly towards her. 'A very romantic lady,' he explained as he drew level with an open-mouthed Jane, dressed casually in denims and a black shirt, the latter worn beneath a grey jacket. 'She was only too happy to let me in when I explained I was your fiancée from America, and that I had come over to surprise you!'

Jane was still stunned at actually seeing him standing here in the hallway, let alone able to take in what he was actually saying.

But the words finally did penetrate her numbed brain, and with that comprehension came anger at the way he'd managed to trick his way in. And she was already angry enough that he was here at all! This was her home, her private sanctuary, and no one invaded it. And certainly not Gabriel Vaughan.

Never Gabriel Vaughan...!

She looked at him with coldly glittering eyes. 'Take your flowers, Mr Vaughan,' she bit out in a heavily controlled voice, 'and—'

'I hope you aren't about to say something rude, Jane,' he cut in mockingly.

'And yourself,' she finished hardly, breathing deeply in her agitation, two spots of angry colour in her cheeks. 'And leave. Before I call the police and have you thrown out!' she added warningly as he would have spoken. 'I have no idea how you found out where I actually live, but—'

'I've hired a car for my stay over here; the weather was so bad the other evening, I decided to follow you home, to make sure you got back okay,' he explained softly, his eyes narrowed on her as he saw all too easily how angry and upset she was.

He might be able to see it, but he was also going to hear it! 'Your behaviour, Mr Vaughan, is bordering on harassment,' she bit out tartly. 'And if it continues I certainly will make a complaint to the police.' Even as she repeated that threat, she knew that she would do no such thing.

The police had been involved three years ago, calling at her home, poking and prying into her personal life, into Paul's life—There was no way she would willingly open herself up to that sort of turmoil again, and certainly not with Gabriel Vaughan once again at its centre!

Gabe gave a pained grimace. 'I only wanted to make sure you got home safely in that awful weather,' he excused challengingly.

Jane glared at him. 'I don't believe you! And after I've explained your other behaviour I don't think the police would either!'

'Aren't you taking this all a little too seriously, Jane?' He attempted to cajole her, shaking his head teasingly.

He had followed her home the other evening so that he knew where she lived, had tricked his way into her apartment building today on the pretext of bringing her flowers but actually so that he could be here waiting for her when she got home; no, she didn't think she was overreacting at all!

'Evie—the lady in the apartment below,' she explained impatiently at his puzzled look, 'may have found your actions romantic, Mr Vaughan...' The other woman had been trying to find out from Jane for months if there was a man in her life; Evie was involved with a married man herself, which was how she was able to live in the apartment she did. 'I, on the other hand,' Jane added hardly, 'find them completely intrusive. If I had wanted you to know where I lived then I would have told you!'

His mouth twisted ruefully. 'Don't you have any sympathy at all for a lone male in a foreign country?'

Jane gave him a disgusted look. 'Not when that "lone male" could have women queuing up outside his door to keep him company!'

He raised dark brows. 'I prefer to choose my own female company,' he drawled.

'Me?' Jane sighed scathingly.

'In a word—yes,' Gabe nodded. 'Jane, you're bright, funny, independent, run your own very successful business, and you're very, very beautiful,' he added huskily.

She swallowed hard. It was so long since any man had spoken to her like this, had told her she was beautiful. It had been her decision, she accepted that, but why, oh, why did that man now have to be Gabriel Vaughan?

'As opposed to?' she prompted dryly, sure she couldn't be that unique in his acquaintance.

He grimaced. 'Oh, undoubtedly beautiful,' he conceded. 'But also vacuous, self-oriented, self-centred, and usually having no other thought in their head other than marrying a rich man. So that they can continue to be vacuous, self-oriented, et cetera, et cetera,' he concluded harshly.

He had just, from what little Jane knew of the other woman, exactly described the woman who had been his wife—Jennifer Vaughan, she'd been tall, beautiful, elegant—and totally selfish!

Jane sighed, closing her eyes briefly before looking at him once again. 'Gabe—'

'That's the first time you've dropped the Mr Vaughan.' He pounced, sensing some sort of victory. 'Do you have the makings of dinner in here?' He took the two bags of shopping out of her arms before she could stop him, looking in at the contents. 'Spaghetti bolognese,' he guessed accurately seconds later. 'I could make the sauce while you see to the pasta,' he offered lightly.

'You—'

'Let someone else cook for you for a change, Jane,' he prompted determinedly. 'I make a mean bolognese sauce,' he promised her.

She did a mental inventory of her apartment as she had left it a couple of hours ago: tidy, comfortably so, but also impersonal, no incriminating photographs, absolutely nothing to show the woman she had once been...

And then she brought herself up with a start. She wasn't seriously contemplating taking Gabriel Vaughan into her home, was she?

That was exactly what she was thinking!

What magic had this man worked on her that she could even be considering such an idea? Perhaps it was that 'lone male' remark, after all...? She, of all people, knew just how miserable, how desolate loneliness could be...

'No standing around just watching me work once we're inside,' she warned as she picked up the flowers before unlocking the door and going inside.

She strode through, giving him little time to look around her open-plan lounge. The large kitchen was wood-panelled, with herbs and spices hanging from the ceiling, pots and pans shining brightly as they hung from hooks placed over the table in the centre of the room—an old oak table that she had bought in an auction at a manor house, its years of constant use meaning it was scored with cuts and scratches, some of which Jane had added herself in the last year.

'Exactly as I imagined it,' Gabe said slowly as he looked around admiringly.

How he had 'imagined it'...? Since when had he started imagining what her home looked like?

'Since that first night at Felicity and Richard's.' He lightly answered the accusing question in her eyes. 'You can tell a lot about a person from their home.'

Which was probably the reason why she never brought anyone here! She didn't want anyone to be able to 'tell' anything about her—

'This is the kitchen of a chef,' Gabe announced happily, starting to unpack the shopping bags. 'Everything you could possibly need to cook.' He indicated the numerous pots and pans. 'The knives all sharp.' He pulled one neatly from the kniferack. 'And a bottle of red wine—room temperature, of course!—to sip and enjoy while we cook.' He looked at her enquiringly as he held up the bottle that already stood on the table.

He was right; she had left the wine out so that it would be exactly the right temperature for drinking when she returned home to prepare her meal. But this to 'enjoy while we cook' sounded a little too—cosy, intimate. Everything she was hoping to avoid where this man was concerned.

'Lighten up, Jane,' Gabe advised laughingly as he read the indecision in her expression, deftly removing the cork from the bottle of wine as Jane busied herself putting the flowers in water. 'I was suggesting we share a bottle of wine—not a bed!' He slipped off his jacket, placing it on the back of one of the kitchen chairs.

Jane put the vase of flowers down on the window-ledge with a thump. 'You'll find the glasses in the cupboard over there.' She nodded abruptly across the kitchen.

Share a bed, indeed! She hadn't shared a bed with any man since—She shuddered just at the thought of having once shared a bed with Paul!

Luckily she was concentrating on preparing the pasta by the time Gabe came back with the wine glasses, her shudder of revulsion unseen by him. Otherwise he might have wanted to know just why a woman of twenty-eight, obviously healthy, and not unattractive, should shudder at the mere thought of such intimacy…!

Gabe sliced up the onion with one of her sharp knives, and Jane couldn't help but admire the way he diced it into small pieces, ready for sautéing in the butter he had gently melting in a frying pan on top of the Aga. And he was obviously enjoying himself too, perfectly relaxed, humming softly to himself as he worked.

Strange; she had always thought of Gabriel Vaughan as an over-tall man, powerfully built, his face set into grimly angry lines. And this man, grinning to himself as he fried onions, didn't fit into that picture at all…!

He turned to take a sip from the nearest of the two

glasses of wine he had poured out for them. 'This is fun, isn't it?' He smiled widely at her.

Jane's smile was much more cautious; she had a feeling a little like having been swept over by a tornado, not even sure how the two of them had come to be in her kitchen cooking a meal together. He was the very last man she would have thought she would spend any time with!

'Jane?' he prompted softly at her silence, no longer smiling, frowning at her lack of response.

It was the disappearance of that smile that affected her the most; it had been a completely natural smile, without cynicism or innuendo. He really had been enjoying himself a moment ago as he'd cooked the onions!

And now she felt guilty for upsetting his pleasure...

'You dealt with that onion very professionally,' she told him lightly, taking a break to sip her own wine. 'At a guess, I would say it's something you've done before!' she added teasingly.

'Dozens of times,' he nodded, that light note back in his voice as he turned to toss the onions in the butter. 'I've always liked to cook at home,' he shrugged. 'Although I have to admit I haven't done so for some time.' He frowned at the realisation. 'Jennifer—my wife— didn't think it was worth bothering to eat at all if there was no one to see her doing it,' he added ruefully.

His wife. Jennifer. How the very sound of that name had once hurt her! But now she'd heard it, from the man who had been her husband, and she felt nothing, not even the numbness that had once been so necessary to her.

'There was you,' she told Gabe dismissively, suddenly busy with the pasta once again.

'There was me,' he echoed self-derisively, tipping in the minced steak to cook with the onions. 'Unfortunately,

Jennifer was the type of woman who was more interested in what other women's husbands thought of her rather than what interested her own husband!'

Jane hadn't even been aware of holding the knife in her hand, let alone how she came to slice her finger with it, but suddenly there was blood on the work surface in front of her, and, she realised belatedly, a stinging pain on the index finger of her left hand.

How ironic, she thought even through the pain, that it should be her left hand that she had cut. The hand that had once worn her wedding ring...

'It was something I— Hell, Jane!' Gabe suddenly saw the blood too, taking the frying-pan off the heat before rushing over to her side, pressing her finger to stop the flow of blood. 'What the hell happened?' He barked his concern. 'Do you think it's bad enough to need stitches? Perhaps I should call—'

'Gabe,' Jane cut in soothingly—she was the one with the cut finger, but he was definitely the one who was panicking! 'It's only a tiny cut. A hazard of the trade,' she added lightly, deliberately playing down the problem this cut would give her over the next busy few weeks. Preparing food, having her hands constantly in and out of water—this cut, even though it really wasn't very serious, would cause her deep discomfort for some time to come.

Damn; she couldn't remember the last time she had done anything this silly. Of course, it had been Gabe's comments about his wife that had caused her lapse in concentration...

'You'll find some plasters in the cupboard over the dishwasher,' she told him abruptly, moving to wash the cut under cold water as he went to get the plasters, the stinging pain in her hand helping to relieve some of the shock she had felt at hearing him discuss his wife so casually.

Gabe deftly applied the plaster once her finger had been dried. 'I don't have a wife any more, Jane,' he told her softly, his gaze searching as he looked down into her face.

He believed it was the thought of having dinner with a potentially married man that had caused her to have this accident! Perhaps it was better that he should continue to think that was the reason...

'I'm glad to hear it,' she dismissed lightly. 'Because if you did,' she added as she saw the light of triumph in his eyes, 'Evie—the woman downstairs—' she reminded him who had let him into the building—and why, '—would be devastated. It would blow all her romantic illusions out of the window!'

'I see,' he sighed, nodding abruptly, before turning his attention back to his bolognese sauce. 'My wife died,' he rasped harshly, no longer looking at Jane.

Because the memory of Jennifer's death must still be a painful one for him, Jane acknowledged. She should know, better than most people, that a person didn't necessarily have to be nice to have someone fall in love with them.

And Jennifer Vaughan had not been a nice woman: tall, beautiful, vivacious, and ultimately dangerous, with a need inside her to bewitch every man she came into contact with, while at the same time eluding any ownership of herself. Only one man had succeeded in taming her even a little. Gabriel Vaughan. And from the little he had so far said about Jennifer, and from what Jane already knew from her own experience, that ownership had been bitter-sweet—and probably more bitter than sweet!

But there could be no doubting that, despite all her faults, Gabe had loved his wife—

'Jennifer was a bitch,' he bit out suddenly, those aqua-blue eyes piercing in their intensity now as he turned back to hold Jane's gaze. 'Beautiful, immoral, whose only pleasure in life seemed to be to destroy what others had built,' he told Jane grimly. 'Like a child with a pile of building bricks another child may have taken time and care to put in place; Jennifer would knock it all down, with an impish grin and a flash of her wicked green eyes!'

Jane swallowed hard. She didn't want to hear any of this! 'Gabe—'

'Don't worry, Jane,' he bit out derisively. 'The only reason I'm telling you this is so that you know I'm not about to launch into some sorrowful tale about how wonderful my marriage was—'

'But you loved her—'

'Of course I loved her!' he rasped, reaching out to grasp the tops of Jane's arms, his gaze burning with intensity now. 'I married her. Maybe that was my mistake, I don't know.' He shook his head impotently. 'The excitement was all in the chase to Jennifer.' His mouth twisted. 'A loving captive was not what she wanted!'

'Gabe, I really—'

'Don't want to hear?' He easily guessed her cry of protest. 'Well, that's just too bad, because I intend telling you whether you want to know or not!' he told her savagely.

'But why?' Jane choked, looking up at him imploringly, her face pale, eyes dark brown. 'I've asked you for nothing, want nothing from you. I don't want anyone—'

'You don't want anyone disturbing the life you've

made for yourself in your ivory tower,' he acknowledged grimly. 'Oh, I'll grant you, it's comfortable enough, Jane.' He looked about him appreciatively. 'But, nevertheless, it's still an ivory tower. And I'm giving you notice that I intend knocking down the walls—'

'Doesn't that make you as destructive as you just described your wife?' Jane cut in scornfully, her whole body rigid now, standing as far away from him as his grasp on her arms would allow.

Because those fingers were like steel bands on her flesh, not hurting, but at the same time totally unmoveable. The only way to distance herself from him was verbally, to hurt him as his words were hurting her.

'Late wife, Jane,' he corrected her harshly. 'Past tense. And no, it doesn't make me like Jennifer at all. I'm not out to destroy for destruction's sake. I want to build—'

'For the couple of months or so you claim you're going to be in England?' she came back disgustedly, shaking her head. 'I don't think so, thank you, Gabe. Why don't you try Celia Barnaby?' she scorned. 'I'm sure she would be more than happy to—'

Her words were cut off abruptly as Gabe's mouth came crashing down on hers, pulling her into the hardness of his body, knocking the breath from her lungs as he did so, rendering her momentarily helpless.

And Gabe took full advantage of that helplessness, his mouth plundering, taking what he wanted, sipping, tasting the nectar to be found there. And then finally the onslaught ceased, Gabe having sensed her lack of response.

He began to kiss her gently now, his hands moving to cradle either side of her face as his lips moved caressingly against her own, that gentleness Jane's undoing.

She began to respond…!

Something deep, deep inside her began to break free at the softly caressing movement of Gabe's lips against hers, a yearning for something she had denied herself for the last three years, a warming to an emotion she hadn't allowed in her life for three years.

But Gabe didn't love her. And she certainly didn't love him. And anything else they might be able to give each other would be totally destroyed the moment he discovered who she really was...!

Gabe raised his head slightly, his hands still cradling each side of her face, his eyes glittering down into hers, but not with anger now—with another emotion entirely. 'I'm not interested in Celia Barnaby, Jane,' he told her huskily. 'In any way. The only reason I was anywhere near her home at all the other evening was because I knew you would be there,' he admitted self-derisively.

It was as she had guessed, but hoped wasn't true. Gabe had to have been one of those extra guests Celia had telephoned her about—and it had been by his own design.

'I want you, Jane—'

She pulled sharply away from him, breathing easier once she was free. 'You can't have me, Gabe,' she told him dully. 'Because I don't want you,' she added as he would have protested, his expression grim now. 'I realise it must be difficult for the eligible Gabriel Vaughan to accept that a woman may not want him, but—'

'Cut the insults, Jane,' he put in scathingly. 'I heard what you said the first time around! What is it about you, Jane?' he added with a shake of his head as he took in her appearance from head to toe, her hair slightly dishevelled now from his caressing fingers, her eyes twin pools of sherry-brown in the paleness of her face. 'I've wanted you since the moment I first set eyes on you! Not only that,' he continued harshly. 'but I've found myself thinking more—and now talking, too—about the wife I've tried to put from my mind for three years. Why is that, do you think, Jane?' His eyes glittered with anger once again, but it was impossible to tell whether that anger was directed at Jane or himself.

She knew exactly why she had thought more of the past, of Paul, her own dead husband, this last week. Gabriel Vaughan, with his own involvement in that death, had brought back all the unwanted memories she had mainly succeeded in pushing to the very back of her mind. And part of Gabe, Jane was beginning to realise— although it was only subconsciously in him at the moment—recognised something in her, evoking his own thoughts and memories of the past.

How long before those subconscious memories became full awareness…?

'I really have no interest in learning why, Gabe,' she told him dismissively. 'And that's something I do know the answer to—I'm not interested in you!' She looked across at him with cold challenge, her heart pounding loudly in her chest as she waited for his reaction.

He predictably met that challenge, his gaze unwavering. 'You know damn well that isn't true—and so do I!' he bit out harshly. 'Whoever he was, Jane—' he shook his head '—he certainly isn't worth hiding yourself away—'

'In my ivory tower?' she finished scornfully, angry with herself and him—for the tell-tale colour that had appeared in her cheeks when he had challenged her denial of being interested in him. Because he had breached the barriers she had erected around her emotions, no matter how briefly… 'Was Jennifer worth it?' she returned pointedly.

His brows arched, his mouth twisting ruefully. 'Neatly turned, Jane,' he drawled admiringly. 'But completely ineffective; Jennifer, and anything she may have done while she was alive, lost the power to hurt me long ago,' he assured her disgustedly.

'How about the pain she caused when she died?' Jane returned harshly.

And then wished she hadn't as she saw Gabe's gaze narrow speculatively. She was becoming careless in her own agitation with this situation...!

'She died in a car accident, Jane,' Gabe said softly. 'And there's nothing more final than death,' he added harshly. 'Dead people can't hurt you.'

'Can't they?' she breathed huskily.

He gave a firm shake of his head. 'If Jennifer hadn't died when she did, I think I would one day have ended up strangling her myself! So you see,' he added scathingly, 'the only thing Jennifer did when she died was save me the trouble of doing the job myself!'

It wasn't. Jane knew it wasn't. And, no matter how bitter he might now have become about his wife's past behaviour, so did Gabe. Because three years ago, after the car accident in which Jennifer died, Gabe had been like a man demented, had needed to blame someone, and with the death of the only person he could blame he had turned his anger and humiliation onto the only person left in the whole sorry mess that he could still reach...!

Gabe was right when he guessed a man was responsible for her living in an emotional fortress, what he chose to call her 'ivory tower'.

It was the same man who was partly responsible for

her becoming plain Jane Smith.

The same man she had been hiding her real self away from for the past three years.

And that man was Gabriel Vaughan himself!

CHAPTER SIX

'DON'T look so worried, Jane,' he taunted now. 'Those murderous feelings were only directed towards my wife; I actually abhor violence!'

So did she. Oh, God, so did she. But, nevertheless, she was no stranger to it...

'It's said there's a very fine line between love and hate,' she said dully.

And she knew that too. She had been so in love with Paul when she'd married him, but at the end of four years she had hated him. For what he had done to her family. And for what he had taken from her.

But she also knew, no matter how difficult to live with, how selfish Jennifer had been, that Gabe had loved his wife. That he had loved her enough to seek out the people he felt were involved in her death...

'Shouldn't we finish cooking this meal?' Gabe suddenly suggested with bright efficiency, placing the frying-pan back on top of the Aga.

Jane continued to look at him dazedly for several long seconds. She had no interest in cooking the meal, let alone eating it, not after what had been said. Or the way Gabe had kissed her minutes ago... She wasn't even sure she could eat after that!

'Come on, Jane,' Gabe said briskly. 'The food will do us both good.' He turned away again, as if what he had just said settled the matter; they would eat dinner together.

Because he was a man used to giving orders. And having them carried out.

But Jane didn't finish cooking the spaghetti for either of those reasons. Quite simply, when she cooked, created, she could forget all that was going on around her. And, after thinking of her marriage to Paul, it was very necessary that she do that at this moment.

'Excellent!' Gabe pronounced with satisfaction a short time later, having almost finished eating the spaghetti bolognese on his plate. The two of them were seated at the huge oak dining table, their glasses replenished with the red wine, the remaining food still steaming hot on their plates. 'Maybe the two of us should go into business together,' he added in a challengingly soft voice.

Jane gave him a sharp look, knowing by the teasing glitter in his eyes that he was looking for a reaction from her. 'I don't think so,' she came back dismissively. 'Somehow I don't see you working for anyone!'.

Dark brows rose. 'I was thinking more along the lines of a partnership,' he drawled.

She gave an acknowledging inclination of her head—she was well aware of exactly what he had meant! 'And I was thinking more along the lines of the clients I work for!'

Gabe laughed softly, forking up some more of his food. 'Why a personal chef, Jane, as opposed to the restaurant Felicity suggested the other evening?' he asked interestedly. 'Surely a restaurant would mean more customers, more—'

'Overheads,' she finished for him. 'More people working for me. Just more complications altogether,' she shrugged dismissively.

Although she had to admit that, at the time she'd begun her business it hadn't been for those reasons that she had chosen to go alone. There had been no money to invest in such a risky venture as opening up her own restaurant. Three years ago she had been left with only one commodity she could use—herself. And her talent at cooking had seemed by far the best course for her to take! Even then it had been a painful year of indecision before that option had occurred to her.

'And you're a person that likes to avoid complications, aren't you?' Gabe said shrewdly.

She returned his narrow-eyed gaze unblinkingly. 'With only myself to rely on, I felt I stood a better chance of success.' She deliberately didn't answer his question.

'But what about now?' Gabe continued conversationally. 'You've already effectively built up your clientele; it wouldn't take too much to—'

'Not everyone is as ambitious as you are, Gabe,' she cut in firmly. 'Three years ago I didn't even have my business—'

'What happened three years ago?' he interrupted softly. 'Just curiosity, Jane,' he assured her as she gave him a startled look. 'Maybe I phrased the question badly,' he conceded ruefully as she still didn't answer. 'Perhaps I should have asked what it was you did *before* three years ago?'

Until the age of eighteen she had been at school. And at eighteen, instead of going to university, she had chosen to go to France, where she had taken an advanced cookery course. At twenty, a few months after her return home, she had met Paul and they'd become engaged. At twenty-one she was married. And at twenty-five she was widowed. The details of those four years as Paul's wife she preferred not to think about!

And she intended telling Gabriel Vaughan none of those things, wished now that she hadn't mentioned 'three years ago' at all. Because it was exactly that length of time since his wife had died...

'I kept busy,' She was deliberately noncommittal, studiously avoiding that searching aqua-blue gaze. 'But I had always wanted to run my own business.' Instead of living in someone else's shadow, always having to tell them how wonderful they were, how successful, how— How *deceitful*!

'And now you have it,' Gabe acknowledged lightly. 'Is it as much fun as you thought it would be?'

Fun? She hadn't ever expected it to be 'fun'. She had wanted independence, freedom, hadn't looked for anything else. And her business had certainly given her those things; she answered to no one!

'There's more to life than success, Jane,' Gabe added at her lack of reply.

'Such as?' she challenged scornfully; he wasn't exactly unsuccessful himself, so how could he be a judge of that?

He shrugged. 'Love,' he suggested huskily.

Jane gave a derisive laugh. 'I don't see how you can possibly say that when you obviously had a love/hate relationship with your own wife!'

His mouth tightened. 'Jennifer did not make me happy,' he conceded. 'But I thought I'd found the perfect woman,' he rasped, his thoughts all inwards now. 'And then she just evaporated, disappeared before my eyes.' He looked across at Jane with pained eyes. 'I haven't been able to look at another woman since without seeing her image imprinted there. At least,' he added gruffly, 'I hadn't. Until six days ago.'

'What happened—? Oh, no, Gabe,' she dismissed scathingly as she realised he was talking of his initial meeting with her. 'Does this chat-up line usually work?' she added disgustedly.

'It isn't a chat-up line,' he told her steadily. 'You know that. And so do I,' he added evenly, keeping his gaze fixed on hers.

It was that steady gaze that made her realise he meant every word he was saying!

'You're being ridiculous, Gabe,' she bit out agitatedly. 'You can't be attracted to me!'

He tilted his head thoughtfully to one side. 'That's a very interesting way of putting it.'

Again she realised her mistake too late; it was an 'interesting way of putting it'. And she knew exactly why she had said it that way. But the last thing she wanted was for Gabe to know that reason!

'I'm just not your type,' she said impatiently.

Those dark brows rose again. 'Do I have a type?' he drawled in amusement.

Jane sighed. 'Of course you do,' she snapped irritably. 'You've always been attracted to tall, elegant blondes. You married a tall, elegant blonde! Whereas I—' She broke off, having realised by the widening of his eyes that she had once again said too much.

She just couldn't seem to help it where this man was concerned. She simply wasn't any good at playing the sophisticated games that people like Gabe—and Paul— liked to play. It was one of the reasons Paul had become so bored with her; he had been sure that the doting daughter and equally doting fiancée were an act, had been furious after their marriage to learn that that was exactly what she was. Her shyness annoyed him, her total love irritated him, and as for the doting daughter—!

It had become a marriage made in hell, her shyness turning to coldness as a way of protecting herself from Paul's taunts; her total love had deteriorated to pity that he obviously wasn't able to feel such emotion himself.

And the 'doting daughter' had kept all her pain and misery to herself, in an effort to spare her parents the heartache of knowing she had made a terrible mistake in marrying Paul!

'You're a short brunette,' Gabe conceded dryly. 'Which makes a mockery of the tall blonde.' His eyes narrowed. 'How did you know my wife was blonde? I'm sure I didn't mention it...'

There was an underlying edge of steel to his tone that hadn't been there before, and Jane realised that a lot depended on her next answer. 'Celia Barnaby insisted on talking to me about you the other evening,' she told him truthfully, relieved to see some of the tension ease out of his stiffly held shoulders. And it was the truth—except Celia hadn't told her his wife was a blonde either! But if what he had told her about Celia was true, then he was never likely to find that out from the other woman, was he? 'I believe the implication was that, being tall and blonde herself, she was worthy of your interest,' Jane added mockingly.

He shrugged, relaxed once more. 'I seem to have lost my appetite for tall blondes,' he returned dryly.

Then it was a pity her hair wasn't its natural honey-blonde; it would have nullified her attraction on one count, at least! But if her hair had still been blonde Gabe would probably have instantly recognised her, anyway. And that would never do!

'Celia assures me that blondes have more fun,' Jane derided, having no intention of explaining to him the circumstances under which the other woman had made that remark! She was still unnerved herself at the other woman's realisation of her real hair colour...

'If you like that sort of fun.' Gabe's mouth twisted

scornfully. 'I don't. How old are you, Jane?' He abruptly changed the subject.

She blinked, seeming to have averted one catastrophe—but unsure whether or not she was heading for another one! 'Twenty-eight,' she supplied with a frown.

He nodded, as if it was about what he had already guessed. 'And I'm thirty-nine.'

She shook her head. 'I don't see—'

'Because I hadn't finished,' he told her with mild rebuke. 'I'm thirty-nine years old, was married, and now I'm not. I'm a wealthy man, can do what I like, when I like—pretty much as you can, I imagine,' he acknowledged ruefully. 'The difference being,' he continued as she would have spoken, 'that for me it isn't enough. When my wife died three years ago— Strange that your life seems to have changed around that time too...?' he added thoughtfully.

Jane held her breath as she waited for him to continue. If he did. Oh, please, God, don't let him pursue that subject!

He shrugged, as if it was something he would go back to another time; right now he was talking about something completely different. 'When Jennifer died all my illusions died along with her,' he continued harshly. 'And that illusion of perfection disappeared too.'

Not surprising, in the circumstances! He must have really loved Jennifer to have ever thought she was perfect! But then, hadn't Jane made the same mistake about Paul...? Love, it appeared, made fools of them all!

'Or so it seemed,' Gabe added softly, looking pointedly at Jane.

He didn't seem the type of man who fell victim to infatuations, and yet the way he was looking at her...! Maybe she had formed completely the wrong impression of this man, because at this moment that was exactly how he was behaving!

'I can assure you, I'm far from perfect,' she told him firmly, standing up to clear away her plate, the food only half eaten, but the evening over as far as she was concerned. 'I wish you luck in your search for this perfection, Gabe,' she added dismissively. 'But count me out. I don't meet the criteria, and, even more important, I happen to like my life exactly the way it is.' Her eyes flashed a warning.

Because she did like her life the way it was. She was her own boss, both privately and professionally, could pick and choose now what she would and wouldn't do. And she had deliberately planned for it to be that way. And it was how she intended it to stay.

Gabe clearly saw that warning in her eyes, standing up too. 'Don't you ever long for anything different, Jane? Marriage? Children?' he persisted.

Jane felt the pain only briefly, bringing a shutter down over her emotions, her gaze impenetrable as she looked at him coldly. 'Like you, Gabe, I've tried the former,' she bit out between stiff lips. 'And I also know it isn't necessary for the latter,' she added flatly. 'And no, I don't long for either of those things.' Not again. Not ever again. She belonged to herself, would never be owned by anyone ever again.

Gabe looked at her through narrowed lids. 'You've been married?'

Once again this man had provoked her into saying too much. Far, far too much. She seemed to head him off from one direction, only to find he was going in another one that was just as intrusive.

'Hasn't everyone?' she dismissed with deliberate carelessness. 'With the divorce rate as high as it is, surely it's inevitable!' she added scathingly.

That aqua-blue gaze remained narrowed on her thoughtfully. And Jane hadn't missed that glance he had briefly given her left hand. But he would find no tell-tale signs of a ring having been worn there, no indentation, no paler skin from a summer tan; her ring had been consigned to a river long ago. Along with all the painful memories that went with it.

'You're divorced?' Gabe probed softly now.

Oh, no, he wasn't going to get any more information out of her that way!

'My father told me you should try everything once,' she answered mockingly. 'And if you don't like it the first time then don't repeat the experience!' Once again she didn't actually answer his question, and she knew by the rueful expression on his face that he was well aware of the fact, that it was yet another subject he would store away for the moment to be returned to on another occasion.

And he would be wasting his time, now and in the future; she had no intention of answering any of his questions about her marriage!

'Do your parents live in London?'

She drew in a gasping breath—this man just didn't give up, did he!

'No,' she answered unhelpfully. 'Do yours live in America?'

His mouth twisted in acknowledgement of her having turned the question back to him. 'They do,' he drawled dryly, the two of them having cleared the table now. 'In Washington DC. My dad was in politics, but he's retired now.'

If he thought that by appearing open about his own

family she would return the compliment, then he was mistaken! 'Do politicians ever retire?'

'Not really.' Gabe smiled at the question. 'But it's what he likes to tell people. He and Mom have been married for forty years.'

And her own parents had been married for thirty. In fact, tomorrow was their wedding anniversary, and she intended going to see them for a few hours on Saturday. Sadly a few hours was all she could bear nowadays.

It used to be so different, her parents doting on their only child. But what Paul had done three years ago had affected them all, and now her father was a mere shadow of his former self, and her mother desperately tried to keep up a pretence for Jane's benefit that everything was normal whenever she went to see them. But Jane wasn't fooled for a minute, and her visits, few and far between nowadays, were as much of a strain for her as they were for her parents.

'Someone should give them a medal,' she told Gabe cynically. 'A lasting marriage seems to be a dying art!'

'That isn't true,' he defended. 'There are lots of happily married couples. Look at Felicity and Richard,' he pointed out triumphantly.

'You didn't,' Jane reminded him dryly. 'You accused me of having an affair with Richard!'

Gabe grimaced. 'A natural mistake, in the circumstances.'

Jane gave him a look of exasperation. 'And just what "circumstances" would they be?'

He shrugged uncomfortably. 'You were very strong in your defence of him.'

Because of her past knowledge of Gabe, not because she was actually close to the other couple. Although she did like Felicity and Richard, admired their happy mar-

riage and beautiful daughters. And it had been the destruction she knew this man could wreak that had made
her defend them so fiercely. It seemed that defence had
succeeded in arousing Gabe's suspicions, but in completely the wrong direction—thank goodness!

'It's an English trait,' she answered dryly. 'We always
root for the underdog,' she explained at Gabe's puzzled
expression.

His mouth twisted ruefully. 'I doubt Felicity and
Richard think of themselves as such!'

'I visited Felicity today.' Jane looked at him pointedly.

He gave that mocking inclination of his head. 'And
she told you about my business deal with Richard,' he
guessed wryly. 'And now part of you—a very big part if
I know anything about you at all—is wondering what I'm
up to now! Will it make any difference if I tell you nothing; it's a straightforward business arrangement, with no
hidden agenda?'

Jane still looked at him sceptically. 'And what's in it
for you?' Because from what Felicity had told her about
that deal, he had gained absolutely nothing. And that
didn't sound like the Gabriel Vaughan she knew at all!

'It means I can sleep nights,' he muttered harshly.

Her eyes widened. 'Don't tell me you have a conscience, Gabe?' she said disbelievingly.

'Is that so hard to believe?' he rasped.

She shrugged; three years ago she wouldn't have believed he had a conscience to bother—and she didn't
want to start changing her opinion of him now! 'I find it
so, yes,' she answered truthfully.

'Oh, it's there, I can assure you,' he bit out. 'And I've
just realised you very neatly changed the subject again a
few minutes ago,' he added mockingly.

Jane looked at him with innocently wide sherry-brown

eyes. She wasn't actually sure which subject he meant; there seemed to be so many of them that she didn't wish to discuss with this man!

Gabe threw back his head and laughed. 'Does that innocent-little-girl expression usually work?' he finally sobered enough to ask.

'Usually—yes.' Jane grinned back at him in spite of herself.

'God, Jane, you're beautiful when you smile!' he said with husky admiration. 'You're also trying to change the subject—again!' he added chidingly.

She arched her brows. 'Am I?'

'Oh, yes,' he acknowledged without rancour. 'Tell me, do you play bridge?'

'As a matter of fact, I do,' she admitted dryly.

'And chess?'

She smiled again, knowing exactly what he was getting at. 'Yes,' she confirmed wryly.

'Unfortunately—for you—so do I!' Gabe drawled teasingly. 'Tell me, Jane, do you believe in love at first sight?' he added softly, his gaze suddenly intense once again.

'No,' she answered without hesitation. 'Not at second, third, or fourth, either!' she bit out tautly.

He frowned at her answer. 'Was your marriage that awful?'

'In its own way. Wasn't yours?' she challenged, once again avoiding talking about her marriage to Paul. 'Awful' didn't even begin to describe it! 'Even loving your wife as you did?'

He sighed heavily. 'Let me tell you about my feelings for Jennifer—'

'Gabe, I don't want to know about your marriage or your wife,' Jane cut in agitatedly; she already knew all she needed to know about both those things. 'If you're still having trouble coming to terms with what happened, and need someone to talk to about it, then I suggest you try a marriage guidance counsellor—or a priest!' she added insultingly, eyes gleaming darkly.

He drew in a sharp breath. 'What the hell do you mean by that?'

'I have no idea,' she sighed wearily. 'But that's my whole point really, Gabe; I have no idea because I don't want to know. How many times do I have to keep saying that?' she added with deliberate scorn.

'I'm obviously a slow learner,' he murmured thoughtfully, picking up his jacket from the back of the chair. 'I thought you were different, Jane.' He frowned. 'I still think that,' he added firmly. 'I also don't think you're as indifferent to me as you would like to think you are.' He shrugged into his jacket. 'Thanks for the meal, Jane. And the conversation. Believe it or not, I enjoyed both!'

She did find that hard to believe. Oh, parts of the evening—very small parts!—had been pleasant, but his kisses had had a devastating effect on the emotional barriers she had succeeded in putting up over the last three years, and the conversation about his wife was something she hadn't enjoyed at all, and she couldn't believe Gabe had enjoyed talking about Jennifer either. And Jane certainly regretted having revealed so much about her own life…

'Thank you for the flowers,' she said stiffly. 'But please don't try and use Evie again to get in here,' she added hardly, eyes glittering warningly. 'She may be a romantic—but I'm not!'

'And you intend putting her straight about your American fiancée,' Gabe guessed easily. 'Next time I come here, Jane, it will be at your invitation,' he promised.

That day would never come, she inwardly assured herself as she walked him to the door.

Gabe turned in the doorway, gently touching one of her pale cheeks. 'I really mean you no harm, Jane,' he told her huskily.

He might not mean to harm her, but he had already shaken the foundations of her new life. 'I wouldn't allow you to,' she assured him firmly.

He gave a wry smile. 'Look after yourself, Jane Smith,' he told her softly. 'Because I very much doubt you would allow anyone else to do so!' came his parting shot.

Jane closed and locked the door before he had even walked down the carpeted hallway to the lift, leaning back against it with a sigh, closing her eyes wearily.

But the action had little effect in closing out the image of Gabe in her apartment, of Gabe kissing her until she responded...

CHAPTER SEVEN

THE house looked the same as it always had as Jane drove down the long driveway. There was snow still on the grass verge and trees, but it had mainly melted on the gravel driveway—evidence that one or both of her parents had driven down it in the last few days.

Jane had always loved this house set in the Berkshire countryside. She'd grown up here from child to teenager in the surrounding grounds and woods. This was her parents' home, where she had only ever known love and the closeness of a happy family.

Although she felt none of that warmth now as she parked her van outside the house. It was no longer the grand house it had once been; the paintwork outside was in need of redoing, and inside only the main parts of the house were kept in liveable order now. The once gracious wings on either side of this were closed up now, being too expensive to heat, let alone keep clean and tidy. There was only Mrs Weaver in the kitchen now to cook and tend the house, a young girl from the village coming in at weekends to help with the heavy housework. Once the house had had a full-time staff of five, and three gardeners to tend the grounds. But not any more. Not for three years now...

Jane got out of her van, taking with her the cake she had made for her parents' anniversary and the bunch of flowers she had bought to signify the occasion. She let herself in through the oak front door, knowing Mrs

Weaver had enough to keep her busy without having to answer the door to the daughter of the house.

Jane paused in the grand hallway, putting down the box containing the cake on the round table there, before looking up at the wide sweep of the staircase, briefly recalling the ball that had been held here for her eighteenth birthday—her walking down that staircase in the beautiful black gown her mother had helped her to choose, with her honey-coloured waist-length hair swinging loosely down her slender back.

At the time it had seemed to Jane she had the whole world at her feet, little dreaming that ten years later her perfect world would have been totally destroyed. And as for her youthful dreams that night of Mr Right and happy-ever-after...! As she had told Gabriel Vaughan two evenings ago, she no longer believed in them, either!

Gabriel Vaughan...

She had tried not to think of him for the last two days, and as she had been particularly busy, catering for a lunch as well as a dinner yesterday, she had managed to do that quite successfully. Although she had to admit she had felt slightly apprehensive about the dinner party the evening before, in case Gabe should once again be one of the guests!

But it had been a trouble-free evening. As the last two days had been Gabriel Vaughan-free. And strangely enough, after his initial bombardment of her privacy and emotions, she found his complete silence now almost as unnerving. What was he up to now...?

'Janette, darling!' her mother greeted warmly as Jane entered the comfortable sitting-room, a fire blazing in the hearth—the only form of heating they had in the house now that central heating was an unaffordable luxury.

Fires were lit each day in this sitting-room and in the master bedroom.

Her mother looked as elegantly beautiful as ever as she rose to kiss Jane, tall and stately, blonde hair perfectly styled, make-up enhancing the beauty of her face. And despite her fifty-one years, and the birth of her daughter, Daphne Smythe-Roberts was still as gracefully thin as she had been in her youth.

It took Jane a little longer to turn and greet her father, schooling her features not to reveal the shock she felt whenever she looked at his now stooped and dispirited body. Ten years older than her mother, her father looked much older than that, no longer the vibrantly fit man he had once been, a force to be reckoned with in business.

Jane forced a bright smile to her face as he too rose to kiss and hug her, over six feet in height, but his stooped shoulders somehow making him appear shorter, the thickness of his hair no longer salt-and-pepper but completely salt, his handsome face also lined with age.

Guilt.

Jane felt overwhelmed with it every time she visited her parents nowadays. If she hadn't fallen in love with Paul, if she hadn't married him, if her father hadn't decided to groom his son-in-law to take over the business from him one day, handing more and more of the responsibility for the day-to-day running of the company to the younger man, at the same time trusting Paul more and more on the financial side of things too... If only. If only!

Because it had been a trust Paul had abused. And as his wife, as his widow, Jane could only feel guilt and despair for the duplicity on Paul's part that had robbed her parents of the comfortable retirement years they had expected to enjoy together.

'You're looking wonderful, darling.' Her father held her at arm's length as he looked at her proudly with eyes as brown as her own.

'So are you,' she answered, more with affection than truth.

Her father had lost more than his business three years ago, he had also lost the self-respect that had made his electronics company into one of the largest privately owned companies in the country. And at fifty-eight he had felt too old—too defeated!—to want to start all over again. And so her parents lived out their years in genteel poverty, instead of travelling the world together as they had once planned to do when her father finally retired.

Guilt.

God, yes, Jane felt guilty!

'I think you're looking a little pale, Janette,' her mother put in concernedly. 'You aren't working too hard, are you, darling?'

Guilt.

Yes, her parents felt that guilt too, but for a different reason. The life Jane had now, catering for other peoples' dinner parties, was not the one they had envisaged for their only and much beloved child. But none of them had been in a financial position three years ago to do more than offer each other emotional support.

Things were slightly better for Jane now, and she did what she could, without their knowledge, to help them in the ways that she was able. Before she left later this afternoon she would deliver to the kitchen such things as the smoked salmon that her mother loved, several bottles of her father's favourite Scotch, and many other things that simply could not be bought in the normal budget of the household as it now was. Her mother, Jane felt, probably was aware of the extras that Jane supplied them with—after all, her mother had always managed the household budget—but by tacit agreement neither of them ever mentioned the luxuries that would appear after one of Jane's visits.

'Not at all, Mummy,' Janette Smythe-Roberts, assured her mother. She'd once been Janette Granger, before she'd thrown that life away along with her wedding ring— Jane Smith, personal chef, taking her place. 'The business is doing marvellously,' she told her. 'It's just a busy time of year. But I'm not here to talk about me.' She smiled, holding out the flowers to her mother. 'Happy Anniversary!'

'Oh, darling, how lovely!' Her mother blinked back the tears as she looked at her favourite lilies and orchids that Jane had picked out for her.

'And this is for you, Daddy.' She handed her father a bottle of the whisky that she wouldn't have to sneak to Mrs Weaver in the kitchen later, her eyes widening appreciatively as she saw for the first time the display of roses on the table in the bay window. 'My goodness, Daddy,' she said admiringly, the deep yellow and white roses absolutely beautiful. 'Did you grow these in your greenhouse?' Rose-growing had become her father's hobby in the last few years, and whenever he couldn't be found in the house he was out in the greenhouse tending his beloved roses.

In years gone by, the house would have been full of flowers, a huge display on the table in the hallway, smaller vases in the sitting-room and dining-room, posies of scented flowers in the bedrooms. But not any more; there were no gardeners now to tend the numerous blooms her mother had needed to make such colourful arrangements.

'I'm afraid not.' Her father grimaced ruefully. 'Would

that I had. Beautiful specimens, aren't they?' he said admiringly.

Beautiful. But if her father hadn't grown them, where had they come from...?

Her parents' circle of friends had narrowed down to several couples they had known from when they were first married, and Jane couldn't imagine any of them had sent these wonderful roses either. There were at least fifty blooms there, and they must have cost a small fortune to buy.

Her parents' sudden change of financial circumstances had had a strange effect on the majority of people they had been friendly with three years ago, most of them suddenly avoiding the other couple, almost as if they were frightened the collapse and financial take-over of David Smythe-Roberts' company might be catching!

So who had given them the roses?

'We had a visitor yesterday, darling.' Her mother's tone was light, but her gaze avoided actually meeting Jane's suddenly sharp one. 'Of course, he didn't realise it was our anniversary yesterday.' Daphne laughed dismissively. 'But the roses are absolutely lovely, aren't they?' she continued brightly.

He? A sense of forboding began to spread through Jane. He! Which he?

Her hands began to shake, and she suddenly felt short of breath, sure she could actually feel the blood starting to drain out of her cheeks as she continued to stare at her mother.

'Oh, Janette, don't look like that!' Her mother moved forward, clasping both of Jane's hands in her own. 'It was perfectly all right,' she assured her. 'Mr Vaughan didn't stay very long—well, just long enough for a cup of tea,' she admitted awkwardly. 'Talking of tea,' she added desperately as Jane looked even more distressed, 'I think I'll ring for Mrs Weaver to bring us all—'

'No!' Jane at last found her voice again.

Mr Vaughan! Her worst fear had come true; it was Gabe who had come here, to her parents' home, bringing those beautiful roses with him.

Why? It was three years ago now; why couldn't he just leave them all alone? Or had he come here to see the results of what he and Paul, between them if not together, had done to her family?

The man she had spent time with this last week didn't seem to be that cruel, and his actions towards Felicity and Richard Warner didn't imply deliberate cruelty either. But if it wasn't for that reason, why had he come here...?

'I'll take these flowers through to the kitchen and put them in a vase,' she told her parents desperately. 'And I'll ask Mrs Weaver for the tea at the same time.' She had to escape for a few minutes, had to try and make some sense out of what was happening. And she needed to be away from her parents to be able to do that.

'Janie—'

'I won't be long, Daddy,' she assured him quickly, his use of his childhood name for her making her want to sit down and cry. Instead she fled from the sitting-room, much to the dismay of her parents, but necessarily for her own well-being.

She drew a deep breath into her lungs once she was out in the hallway, desperately trying to come to terms with what her mother had just said.

Gabe had been here! To her family home. In the house where she had spent her childhood and teenage years.

Why? she inwardly cried again.

She could hear the concerned murmur of her parents'

voices in the room behind her, knew that her reaction had disturbed them. Ordinarily she kept her feelings to herself, felt her parents already had enough to cope with. But hearing of Gabe's visit here had just been too much of a shock, so completely unexpected that this time it had been impossible to hide her emotions from her parents.

But she had to calm herself now, put the flowers in a vase, ask Mrs Weaver to serve tea, and take in to her parents the cake that she had made to celebrate their anniversary. She had to keep everything as normal as possible. After all, her parents had no idea she had met 'Mr Vaughan' again too...

The housekeeper was, as usual, pleased to see Jane, having worked in the house since Jane was a child. The two of them chatted amiably together as Jane arranged the orchids and lilies in the vase, the very normality of it helping her to put things into perspective. Her family would have their tea and cake, and then they could return to the disturbing subject of Gabriel Vaughan; she felt she had to know what Gabe had found to talk to her parents about during his visit. More to the point, she needed to know what her parents had talked to him about!

Her parents seemed relieved at her relaxed mood when she rejoined them, thrilled with the cake she had made them, all of them having a slice of it with the tea the housekeeper brought in a few minutes later.

But they were all just biding their time, Jane knew; she could feel her parents' tension as well as her own.

'You'll stay and have dinner with us, of course, darling?' her mother prompted expectantly a short time later.

Jane grimaced her regret. 'I'm afraid I won't be able to,' she said.

'Another dinner party, Janie?' her father guessed mildly, the regret in his eyes saying she should be attending the dinner party, not cooking it for other people.

'It's almost Christmas, Daddy,' she reminded him, looking pointedly at the festive decorations they had already put up. 'It's my busiest time.'

He sighed heavily. 'You'll never meet anyone stuck in other people's kitchens!'

She didn't want to meet anyone! Besides, she had met someone. She had met Gabriel Vaughan...

'Always the bridesmaid, never the bride, that's me,' she dismissed teasingly. 'But tell me,' she added lightly, 'besides bringing you the roses, what did Gabriel Vaughan come here for?'

Jane had taken a good look around the sitting-room when she'd returned from the kitchen, looking for any incriminating photographs. There were no recent ones of her in here, only ones of her when she was very young, and then at gymkhanas as she went up to collect one of the rosettes she'd often won. And in those she was a round-faced teenager, with long blonde hair, smiling widely into the camera, a brace on her teeth that she had worn until shortly before her sixteenth birthday.

No, there was nothing in this room to indicate that Jane Smith had once been Janette Smythe-Roberts. And not a single thing in the house, she knew, to say she had ever been Janette Granger, Paul Granger's wife. As Jane had done herself, her parents had destroyed anything that would remind them she had ever been married to Paul Granger, and that included disposing of any photographs of them together. Including their wedding photographs.

'I really couldn't say, dear,' her mother answered vaguely. 'He didn't really seem to want anything, did he, David?' She looked at her husband for support.

'No, he didn't.' Jane's father seemed to answer a little too readily for Jane's comfort. 'He just spent a rather pleasant hour here, chatting about this and that, and then he left again.' He shrugged his shoulders.

From the little she had come to know about Gabe, he didn't have 'pleasant hours' to waste chatting! 'Daddy, the man sat back and watched as your company floundered and almost fell, and then he stepped in with an offer you couldn't refuse—literally!' she said exasperatedly. 'How on earth could you have just sat there and taken tea with the man?'

'What happened in the past was business, Janette,' her father answered firmly, showing some of his old spirit. 'And you have to give the man some credit for keeping on most of the original staff and turning the company around.'

She didn't have to give Gabriel Vaughan credit for anything! But then, her parents had no idea of the way the man had tried so relentlessly to hound her down three years ago. Oh, Gabe had asked her parents for her whereabouts too, and in the circumstances her parents had decided she had already been through enough heartache, and had refused to tell him where she was.

That was when the lies had begun, on Jane's part, her guilt taking on the form of protectiveness from any more emotional pain for her parents. They had already suffered enough.

And so her parents simply had no idea of how Gabe had gone to each of her friends in turn with the same question, how for three months she hadn't been able to contact anyone she knew for fear Gabriel Vaughan would get to hear about it and somehow manage to find her.

Her parents weren't even aware that Gabe was part of the reason she had chosen to open her business under the name Jane Smith. They'd believed her when she'd told them it was because she would prefer it that no one realised she had once been Janette Smythe-Roberts. They'd been through too many humiliations themselves concerning their change of financial circumstances not to believe her!

But now Gabe had been here, to their home, and there was just no way that Jane, having come to know him a little better this last week, believed he had simply come here for tea and a pleasant chat!

'You could have done all that yourself if he had backed you financially rather than taken over the company,' she reasoned tautly. He had just done that for Richard Warner; he could have done the same for her father three years ago!

Her father shook his head, smiling sadly. 'Gabriel Vaughan is not a charitable institution, Janette, he's a businessman. Besides, I was almost sixty then—far too old to dredge up the youthful enthusiasm needed to turn the company around.'

Jane bit back her angry retort, knowing that in a way her father was right about Gabe; he hadn't been the one responsible for breaking her father's spirit. The person who had done that was dead, and beyond anyone's retribution.

Paul, her own husband, was responsible for what had happened to her father's company, for all that had happened three years ago.

And now she was back full circle to those feelings of guilt that always assailed her whenever she visited her parents.

'I still think it's very odd for Gabriel Vaughan to have come here,' she muttered.

It was so odd, she decided later on the slow drive home, that she intended, at the first opportunity, to find out exactly what he had thought he was doing by going to see Daphne and David Smythe-Roberts!

'Jane!' Felicity greeted her warmly as she recognised her voice on the other end of the telephone line. 'How marvellous! I was just about to call you.'

'You were?' Jane prompted warily.

It had taken her twenty-four hours of thought, of trying to sit back from the problem, to try and work out how best to approach solving it. And her problem was Gabriel Vaughan. Wasn't it always?

But the problem this time wasn't how to avoid him, but how to meet him again without it appearing as if she had deliberately set out to do so. Not knowing where his rented apartment was, or where he had set up his office for his stay in England, she had been left with only one line of attack: Felicity and Richard Warner.

She had telephoned the other woman with the intention of calling in to see her, and at the same time casually bringing the conversation round to Gabriel Vaughan.

'I was.' Felicity laughed happily. 'I'm feeling so much better now, and Richard and I did so much want to say thank you for all your help—'

'There's no need—'

'So you've already said,' the other woman dismissed lightly. 'We happen to disagree with you. I suggested we invite you out to dinner, but Richard said that was like taking coals to Newcastle! But being a woman I don't think that's the case at all; I know just how nice it is to let someone else do the cooking for a change!'

Felicity was right, of course. Because Jane cooked for a living, most people seemed to think she just threw meals together for herself like the ones she served to them. She didn't, of course, and one of the few luxuries she allowed herself was to occasionally order a take-out pizza!

'It's a lovely thought, Felicity.' She answered the other woman politely. 'But there really is no need. And I have no wish to play gooseberry—'

'Oh, but you won't be; we're going to invite Gabe to make up the foursome!' Felicity announced triumphantly.

Jane wanted to see Gabe, needed to see him—wasn't that the reason for her call in the first place?—but did she really want to sit down and have dinner with the man?

The answer to that was definitely no; the last time the two of them had had dinner together Gabe had kissed her until her legs felt weak! But the other side of the argument was that they wouldn't be alone this time, so there would be no occasion for him to take such liberties. Another positive thing about accepting this invitation was that she wouldn't have organised meeting Gabe again; Felicity and Richard would be their hosts for the evening...

'Jane?' Felicity prompted uncertainly at her continued silence.

She quickly flicked through her business diary that always sat beside the telephone. With only a week to go to Christmas, she really was heavily booked. But she also appreciated she wasn't going to find a better opportunity for meeting Gabe on more neutral ground than this.

Not that she had any idea how she was possibly going to broach the subject of his visit to her parents—or, rather, the Smythe-Robertses—all she could hope was that an opportunity would present itself some time during the evening.

'I only have a cocktail party to cater for on Tuesday

evening,' she told Felicity thoughtfully. 'I just may be able to make dinner for eight-thirty that evening, if that's any good for you and Richard...?' And, of course, Gabriel Vaughan. Because if he wasn't there, the whole evening would, as far as she was concerned, be a complete waste of time.

It wasn't that she didn't appreciate the Warners' invitation, or the reason behind it; it was just that ordinarily there were so many other things she could have done on Tuesday evening—like taking a rest for a few hours.

'Lovely.' Felicity accepted instantly. 'We'll book Antonio's. Shall we call for you? Or perhaps Gabe would—'

'I'll meet you all at the restaurant,' Jane put in quickly, well acquainted with the popular Italian restaurant. 'I can't leave until the people at the cocktail party have gone on to the theatre, so I can't guarantee it will be exactly eight-thirty when I get there.'

She had no intention—no matter how Felicity might still think she was trying to matchmake!—of going to the dinner party as Gabe's partner for the evening, and she didn't want to give that impression by arriving at the restaurant with him.

'As long as you get there eventually,' Felicity said lightly. 'See you Tuesday.' She rang off.

Jane replaced her own receiver much more slowly. She had her wish—she was going to see Gabriel Vaughan again...

She had never thought a time would come when she would willingly place herself in his company!

She only hoped she didn't live to regret it!

CHAPTER EIGHT

'JANE!' Antonio himself came out of his kitchen to greet her when she arrived at the restaurant shortly after eight-thirty on Tuesday evening.

She wasn't deliberately late: she'd been delayed clearing up from the cocktail party. And then she'd had to change before coming here. Luckily she had taken her black dress and shoes with her, and had been able to drive straight to the resturant once she had finished tidying up.

She and Antonio were old friends. Pasta hadn't been something she was too familiar with preparing two years ago, and so she had gone to the expert so that she might learn before opening up her own business. She had spent a month here at the restaurant working in the kitchen at Antonio's side, and despite what she had heard about temperamental Italian chefs—and Antonio was definitely an example of that!—her month here had been highly enjoyable, and by the end of that time she and Antonio were firm friends.

They kissed each other on both cheeks in greeting, Jane grinning up at the handsome Italian. 'I'm meeting Mr and Mrs Warner,' she explained.

Dark brows rose over teasing brown eyes. 'And Mr Gabriel Vaughan,' he added pointedly.

Gabe was here! She hadn't spoken to either Felicity or Richard since the telephone call on Sunday, so she'd had no idea whether or not Gabe had accepted their invitation.

103

Antonio's speculative teasing assured her that not only had he accepted, but he was obviously already here!

'And Mr Gabriel Vaughan.' She dryly echoed Antonio's words. 'Stop grinning like that, Antonio; this is business.' Which wasn't strictly true, but it certainly wasn't pleasure either, not in the way Antonio thought it was!

'Always business with you, Jane.' He held up his hands exasperatedly. 'Although you never came to work in my kitchen dressed like that!' He looked at her admiringly, the black fitted dress showing the slender perfection of her figure, its short length revealing long, shapely legs. She had brushed her hair loosely about her shoulders, having applied some light make-up, and a peach gloss to her lips.

No, she had to admit, she had never come to work in Antonio's kitchen dressed like this…!

And she had delayed going to the table long enough! 'Point me in the right direction, Antonio,' she requested.

'I will do better than that.' He took a firm hold of her elbow. 'Tonight you are the customer, Jane; I will personally show you to your table.'

Having the extremely tall, incredibly handsome proprietor of the restaurant guide her through the diningroom to her table wasn't conducive to the low-profile life she liked to lead, with all eyes turning in their direction. And Jane couldn't even bring herself to look at the three people already seated at the table he took her to, aware that the two men stood up when Antonio pulled back her chair with a flourish for her to sit down.

Antonio paused to pick up one of her hands, bending to kiss the back of it lightly. 'It's wonderful to see you again, Jane,' he told her huskily, devilment gleaming in those dark brown eyes before he turned and walked arrogantly back to his kitchen.

Devil just about described him, Jane decided with affectionate irritation, her cheeks burning with embarrassment. Antonio had deliberately—

'Mutual admiration society?' rasped an all-too-familiar voice.

Jane turned calmly to meet the hard mockery in those aqua-blue eyes, hopefully revealing none of the nervousness she felt at meeting this man again. Nervous, because the last time they had met he had kissed her. And, worse than that, this man had visited her family home, had talked with her parents, and she still had no idea why, or what he had learnt by going there.

'As it happens, Gabe, yes,' she answered him lightly. 'I admire Antonio as a chef immensely. And I believe he respects my ability too,' she added challengingly.

Heavens, Gabe looked so handsome in his black evening suit and snowy white shirt, the dark thickness of his hair lightly brushing the shirt collar. Jane's breath caught in her throat as she returned the steadiness of his gaze.

She had to thrust her trembling hands beneath the table, on the pretext of placing her napkin across her knees, but in reality so that he shouldn't see that shaking of her hands, and speculate as to the reason for it.

Meeting Gabe again, she decided, under any circumstances, was a mistake!

'Good evening, Felicity, Richard.' She turned warmly to the other couple. 'And once again thank you for inviting me.'

'Our pleasure,' Richard assured her warmly, much more relaxed than when Jane had last seen him.

'I had no idea you knew Antonio?' Felicity teased interestedly.

Jane ruefully returned the other woman's smile. But even as she did so she could feel that aqua-blue gaze still on her. Had no one ever told Gabe it was rude to stare? Probably, she acknowledged ruefully, but, as she knew only too well, Gabe was a law unto himself, and would do exactly as he pleased. And at the moment, despite how uncomfortable it might make her feel, it pleased him to stare at her!

'I worked here for a while,' she explained to Felicity; what was the point in doing anything other than telling the truth? She worked for a living, and, no matter how much her parents might hate the fact that she had to do so, it was an irreversible fact! 'It was where I learnt to avoid the flying kitchen utensils,' she recalled ruefully; Antonio's patience was non-existent when it came to his cooking staff!

'Temperamental, is he?' Gabe drawled dismissively.

Once again she calmly returned his gaze. 'Most men are, I've found,' she told him softly.,

'You meant in the kitchen, of course,' Gabe returned challengingly.

She gave a slight inclination of her head. 'Of course,' she agreed dryly.

Gabe chuckled, shaking his head. 'You meant no such thing,' he acknowledged, visibly relaxing as he sat forward, elbows resting on the table-top. 'It's good to see you again, Jane Smith,' he told her huskily.

She wasn't quite sure how she felt about seeing him again! Her pulse rate had definitely quickened at how handsome he looked in his evening suit, so powerfully male. And yet deep inside her was still that fear of what he might, or might not, have learnt on his visit to her parents' home. And at the moment she wasn't sure which emotion was the dominant one!

'How are the flowers?' he prompted softly at her continued silence. 'Or did you give them away to the first person you saw after I left the other evening?' he added self-derisively.

Jane gave Felicity and Richard a self-conscious glance, but they both gave every impression of being engrossed in their menus. Although Jane was sure that Felicity, for one, romantic that she was, was listening avidly to their exchange.

As for the flowers, Jane hadn't been sure initially whether he meant the flowers he had given her or the roses he had given to her parents! Thankfully, his second question had clarified that for her.

'That would have been the height of bad manners, Gabe,' she returned coolly. 'Especially considering all the trouble you went to to give them to me,' she added pointedly.

'Oh, it was no trouble at all, Jane,' Gabe returned huskily, eyes glowing with laughter—at her expense. 'And you did give me dinner afterwards.'

Devil!

She had thought she was meeting him challenge for challenge, but from the grin Felicity shot her way she knew Gabe had definitely won this particular round. 'As I recall,' she said derisively, 'you had to help cook it!'

'It's such fun cooking together, isn't it?' The effervescent Felicity simply couldn't stay out of the conversation any longer. 'We used to do it all the time, didn't we, Richard?' She turned warmly to her handsome husband.

Richard looked up from his menu. 'We still do, if your condition is anything to go by!' he drawled teasingly.

Felicity blushed prettily. 'I was actually talking about cooking together, darling,' she rebuked laughingly.

Jane couldn't help but admire the obvious happiness of this married couple. Felicity was the same age as her, and yet the other woman had a marvellous husband who obviously adored her, two lovely daughters, and a third child on the way.

Jane had longed for those things too once; for a while she'd even thought that she actually had them. Her expression was wistful now as she realised how fleeting that dream had been.

Then she realised Gabe was watching her, dark brows raised questioningly as he saw the different emotions flitting across her face!

She deliberately schooled her features into their usual inscrutable expression. 'Time to order, I think,' she murmured pointedly, smiling up at Vincenzo as he gave her a friendly wink of recognition.

But her own smile wavered and faded as she turned back and found Gabe was still watching her, the harsh expression on his face saying he didn't appreciate her friendly exchange with the waiter one little bit.

Well, what had he expected? She was twenty-eight years old, and just because she was disillusioned with the opposite sex that did not mean that men didn't still flirt with her! Besides, hadn't Gabe himself been doing that since the moment the two of them were introduced?

His scowling expression seemed to say it was okay for him to do it, but not any other man!

Which wasn't very realistic on his part; most men liked to flirt, but that didn't mean they wanted it to go any further than that. And Vincenzo was a prime example of that. Jane knew for a fact that he adored his wife. Besides which, Anna would probably beat her husband to a pulp if he went any further than flirting with another woman!

Gabe's scowl lightened slightly as he saw that Vincenzo spoke to Felicity with the same warmth he had to Jane seconds earlier, Gabe's expression becoming rueful as he turned and saw Jane's mocking one. He shrugged, as if to say, Okay, my mistake.

It wasn't the only mistake he had made, Jane decided irritably. He had no right to feel jealous of the other man in the first place! One bunch of flowers and a home-cooked meal did not give him any rights where she was concerned!

But as the evening progressed, with Felicity and Richard's presence ensuring that it went smoothly, it became more and more obvious to Jane that she still had no idea how to introduce the subject of his visit to her parents. It was impossible to introduce such a delicate subject casually into the conversation. Even Felicity's questions to Gabe on how his work in England was going only elicited a dismissive reply that he was keeping himself busy.

By the end of the evening Jane felt thoroughly frustrated at not being able to find out what she really wanted to know: why Gabe had visited her parents on Friday!

'Did you drive here, Gabe?' Richard asked as they prepared to leave the restaurant. 'Or can Felicity and I offer you a lift home?'

'I was hoping Jane might offer to drive me.' Gabe answered the younger man, but his aqua-blue gaze was fixed compellingly on Jane at she looked up at him sharply. 'I noticed you only drank half a glass of wine with your meal,' he drawled. 'So I guessed you must have driven here yourself.' He added, 'I came by cab.'

With satisfaction, it seemed to Jane. And he noticed too damn much!

But if she did drive him home maybe then she would find the opportunity—? Who was she kidding? There was no way that she could think of to casually introduce the subject of his visit to the Smythe-Robertses' home!

'I'll drive you home,' she offered flatly. After all, with the other couple present, what choice did she have? 'Thank you both for dinner.' She turned to Felicity and Richard. 'I've enjoyed it.'

And she had. The food had been superb, as usual, and with the other couple present the conversation had flowed smoothly too. Even Gabe's annoying presence hadn't jarred too much as, after his initial terseness, he seemed set to be charming for the rest of the evening. And so Jane's only irritation with the evening was that question regarding her parents. And the way things stood she might just have to let that go. If it wasn't repeated, then perhaps it wasn't a problem...?

'Jane!' Antonio left his kitchen for the second time that evening as he came out to hug her goodnight, smiling down at her as he still held her in his arms. 'I have two wonderful new recipes that you would love,' he told her huskily. 'Come in and see me when you have the time, hmm?'

She answered Antonio positively, explaining that it would have to wait until after the New Year now, as she was so busy, all the time aware that Gabe was listening to their conversation with a sceptical glitter in his eyes and a mocking twist to those firm lips.

'Sorry about that,' she apologised dismissively as they walked out to her van, having parted from the other couple, Gabe's hand light on her elbow. 'Antonio and I are old friends.'

'So you explained earlier.' He nodded tersely as she unlocked the doors. "Come and try my recipes" is certainly a twist on 'etchings'!'

Jane turned to give him a cold look once they were seated inside her van. 'Antonio is a married man!' she told him disgustedly.

'And you have no interest in other women's husbands,' Gabe remembered dryly.

'None whatsoever,' she acknowledged stiffly as she turned on the ignition, warming the engine, as well as themselves. The weather outside was still icy cold, although the snow of last week had now disappeared. 'I would never cause another woman that sort of pain!'

Gabe sat back, perfectly relaxed. 'Then it's as well I'm not still married, isn't it?' he said with satisfaction.

Jane made no reply, not quite sure what he meant by that remark—and not sure she wanted to be, either! This man had so many other minuses against her ever becoming involved with him that his being married would have come last on her list of dislikes where he was concerned!

'Perhaps you would care to tell me where I'm to drive you?' she prompted distantly.

'Mayfair.'

Where else? Only the best for this man. After all, he didn't like hotels, did he? Too impersonal—

'I telephoned you over the weekend.'

Jane glanced sharply across at Gabe before instantly returning her attention to the road. She had received no call from him, no more cryptic messages left on her machine from him, either. But then, as she very well knew, he hated those 'damned things'!

She shrugged. 'I did tell you I was very busy in this time leading up to Christmas.'

'It was Saturday afternoon,' he told her evenly. 'I decided that if I waited for you to contact me I would be dead in my coffin and you might—only might, you understand!—turn up for my funeral!' he bit out disgustedly.

A long shot, concerning his funeral, she had to agree! And Saturday afternoon she had been visiting her parents...

'I was out of town,' she told him lightly, her heart once again thudding in her chest. But it was probably the only chance she was ever going to have... 'A thirtieth wedding anniversary,' she told him truthfully. 'In Berkshire. A couple called Smythe-Roberts.' The last was added breathlessly.

Ordinarily she would never have dreamt of talking of her clients to a third party, but as her parents weren't actually clients... This was too good an opportunity to be missed!

'I've met them,' he nodded dismissively. 'Working on a Saturday afternoon, too.' He shook his head. 'You do keep busy,' he teased. 'Turn left here,' he advised softly. 'It's the apartment block on the right.'

Was that it—'I've met them'? She had finally got around to the subject she was really interested in, and he'd dismissed it with just three words!

And it wasn't true that he had only 'met them'. He had visited them only the day before she had, had taken them roses; wasn't the coincidence of that worth mentioning?

Jane was so agitated by his casual dismissal that she only narrowly avoided hitting a Jaguar coming the other way as she drove the van over to the other side of the road and parked outside the building Gabe had indicated.

Well, she wasn't going to give up now, not when they had come so close. 'What a coincidence,' she said lightly.

Gabe's expression was completely blank in the light given off by the street lamp outside. 'My renting an apartment in Mayfair?' He frowned. 'Do you know someone else who lives here?'

Hardly! Maybe once upon a time her friends might have moved in these sorts of circles, as she had herself, but, as with her parents' friends, most of her own had drifted away too with her own change of circumstances.

Besides, was this man being deliberately obtuse? Probably not, she conceded grudgingly as she saw he still looked baffled by her remark.

'I meant that you know the Smythe-Robertses' too,' she explained patiently.

'I think "know" them is probably putting it too strongly,' Gabe dismissed uninterestedly. 'I knew their daughter much better!'

Jane stared at him, her whole body stiffening in reaction. They hadn't even met three years ago, so how on earth could he claim to have known her?

'Daughter?' She forced herself to sound only casually interested—although it was definitely a strain on her nerves. 'I didn't see their daughter when I was there on Saturday.' Well, she hadn't looked in any of the mirrors there, had she?

She was a person who hated lies—being told them and telling them herself—but she was aware she was stretching the truth now, no matter what she might tell herself to the contrary!

'That doesn't surprise me,' Gabe said disgustedly, glancing up at his apartment building. 'Would you like to come in for a nightcap?'

Would she? Not really. And yet if she wanted to continue this conversation with him...

'Just a coffee would be nice,' she accepted. She got out, and locked the van behind them before following Gabe into the building, the man in the lobby ensuring there could be no incidents like the one where Gabe had tricked Evie into letting him go up to her own apartment.

She didn't really want the coffee, found that it kept her awake if she drank it last thing at night. But she wanted to know why Gabe wasn't surprised that Janette Smythe-Roberts hadn't been present at her own parents' thirtieth wedding anniversary...

'Decaffeinated?' Gabe questioned as they entered the plush apartment, switching on the soft glow of lights as he made his way over to the kitchen.

'Thanks,' Jane accepted vaguely, following slowly.

The apartment was gorgeous, with antique furnishings, the brocade paper on the walls looking genuine too. Only the best, Jane thought again.

'Do I take it that you had an involvement with the Smythe-Robertses' daughter?' she prompted teasingly as she joined Gabe in the ultra-modern kitchen.

She knew damn well he hadn't been involved with Janette Smythe-Roberts, but she needed to keep on this subject if she were to get anywhere at all.

'Hardly.' Gabe barely glanced at her as he moved economically about the kitchen, preparing the coffee. 'Spoilt little rich girls have never appealed to me, either!'

Spoilt little—! Jane glared across the room at the powerful width of his back. She might have been over-indulged by her loving parents when she was younger, but marriage to Paul had obliterated any of that. And there was no money now for her to be 'spoilt' with!

And this man, after his visit to her parents' home last

week, must be aware of that...

'The Smythe-Robertses didn't appear overly wealthy to me.' She spoke lightly as Gabe joined her at the breakfast-bar with the coffee.

'Nor me,' he acknowledged tightly. 'But there was plenty of money there three years ago—and I should know, because I bought David Smythe-Roberts's company from him!—so I can only assume the daughter has it all!'

Jane stared at him. Was that really what he thought? That she would have gone off with the money and left her parents living in what was, in comparison to how they had once lived, near poverty?

Didn't this man know of the debts there had been to pay three years ago, of Paul Granger's gambling, of the way he had siphoned money out of the company to supplement his habit?

But even that hadn't been enough for Paul in the end, and he had begun to sign IOUs he hadn't a hope of paying. IOUs that on his death had passed on to his widow. IOUs that, because of Janette's own ill health at the time, her father had paid out of the money he had received for his much depleted company, her parents having decided she had already suffered enough at Paul Granger's hands.

By the time Jane had felt well enough to deal with any of it, it was already too late; her father had already sorted it all out.

Only Gabriel Vaughan's need for vengeance had survived that sorry mess, and the only person left alive to answer that need had been Janette Granger, Paul Granger's widow. So Janette had been the one to come under his vengeful gaze.

Because, at the time of her death, Gabe's wife,

Jennifer, had been leaving him. And the man she had been leaving him for had been Paul Granger, Jane/Janette's own husband...!

CHAPTER NINE

JANE licked suddenly dry lips, frowning darkly. 'You mean that the daughter—'

'Janette Smythe-Roberts, or rather Janette Granger— her married name,' Gabe supplied scornfully.

'Are you saying her parents gave her all their money and left themselves—left themselves—?' How to describe her parents' present financial position? Genteel poverty probably best described it. But 'spoilt little rich girl' did not best describe her!

'Almost penniless, from what I saw last week,' Gabe said much more bluntly. 'According to the parents their daughter now lives abroad.' The disgust was back in his voice. 'Admittedly, she was beautiful—the most beautiful woman I've ever seen—present company excepted, of course—'

'Please, Gabe,' Jane protested weakly in rebuke, still totally stunned by his summing-up of Janette Smythe-Roberts. As for living 'abroad', there was more than one meaning to that word, and she lived in freedom now, not in another country, as Gabe believed!

And beauty was no good, no good at all, if the person who possessed that beauty was as unhappy as she had been married to Paul. Gabe didn't know, couldn't even begin to guess at the hell her marriage had been. Or the pain that had quickly followed his death...

Gabe grinned now in acknowledgement of her rebuke. 'Okay, I'll cut the compliments. But Janette Smythe-Roberts had the perfect face, the perfect body, the most

117

glorious golden hair I've ever set eyes on,' he told her grimly. 'And all that perfection only acted as a shield to the selfishness within. Do you have any idea what she did three years ago, after her husband died, and her father's company was in trouble? No, of course you don't.' He shook his head as he scathingly answered his own question. 'There was simply no sign of the grieving widow, the supportive daughter, because Janette disappeared. Just disappeared!' he repeated disbelievingly.

Jane stared at him, taken aback by the interpretation he had obviously put on that disappearance.

But there had been a very good reason why she hadn't been on show, why she couldn't face the barrage of publicity that accompanied the death of her husband in the company of Gabe's wife; why her parents had shielded her from the worst of their financial ruin.

For, like Felicity Warner now, with her husband Richard in difficulties with his own company, Janette had been pregnant three years ago. And upon learning of Paul's duplicity, of how he had taken money from her father's company to back up his gambling, of his intention of walking out on her, and leaving her father's business in ruins and herself pregnant with their child, she had lost the baby that she had so wanted, her own life also hanging in the balance.

Was that the selfishness of Janette Smythe-Roberts that Gabe referred to...?

Because she hadn't 'disappeared' at all. She'd been in a private nursing home, under the protection of her parents and doctor, until the danger had passed and she had been well enough to go home—not to the home she had shared with Paul, or even her parents' home, but a rented cottage in Devon, far away from prying eyes.

Gabe had simply chosen to put his own interpretation

on how he perceived her disappearance... But he was wrong, so very wrong.

Jane looked at him now. 'Is it still possible to disappear in this day and age?' she derided lightly.

'Thousands do it every year, so I'm told.' Gabe shrugged dismissively. 'And Janette Smythe-Roberts did it so well, no one seems to have seen her since!'

She shook her head. 'I find that hard to believe.'

He shrugged again. 'Nevertheless, that appears to be the case.'

'Appears to be' was certainly correct! 'Has anyone ever tried to find her?' Jane asked.

Gabe grimaced. 'I had some sort of mistaken idea of helping her myself three years ago—'

'You did?' Her surprise wasn't in the least feigned. Help? Gabe hadn't come bearing gifts three years ago, but something else completely! 'I thought you said you weren't involved with her?' She tried to sound teasing, but somehow it came out accusingly...

'I wasn't.' Gabe grimaced again, his gaze warm now as he reached out and lightly touched her hand. 'Do I detect a note of jealousy in your voice, Jane?'

How could she possibly be jealous of herself?

She snatched her hand away as if he had burnt her. 'Don't be ridiculous,' she snapped, standing up. 'I think it's time I was going—'

'I was only teasing you, Jane.' Gabe laughed softly as he too stood up. 'For some reason that's beyond me, we seem to have spent the latter part of this evening discussing a woman you don't even know—and who I haven't set eyes on for three years!' He frowned. 'And we were doing so well until then, too!' he added cajolingly.

That was his interpretation of the evening; until these last few minutes she hadn't even been able to approach the subject that really interested her!

But in a way he was right; talking of Janette Smythe-Roberts and her parents had certainly caused friction in what had, until then, been a lightly enjoyable evening. Surprisingly so, Jane realised. But then, Felicity and Richard had been understandably relaxed after the end of their recent worries, and Gabe had been charming to all of them.

But as she looked up at Gabe now and saw the teasing light in his gaze turn to something much more dangerous she knew it was definitely time she left...

She knew, as Gabe's head lowered and his mouth claimed hers, that she had left it far too late to reach that conclusion...

She wrenched her mouth away from his. 'No, Gabe—'

'Yes, Jane!' he groaned, cradling either side of her face with his hands as he kissed her gently—first her eyes, then her nose, then her cheeks, and finally her mouth again.

It was that gentleness that was her undoing. If he had been demanding, or even passionate, she would have resisted, but he just kissed her again and again with those gently caressing lips.

'That wasn't so bad, was it?' he finally murmured, resting his forehead against hers.

'No...' she confirmed huskily. 'Not bad.' In fact, it had felt too good. And yet she wished he would kiss her again!

He smiled at her, aqua-blue eyes so close to her own as he gazed into those sherry-brown depths. 'How long did you think you could go on hiding, Jane?' he murmured affectionately.

Every alarm bell she possessed went off inside her at

the same time, her eyes widening, her breath catching in her throat, every muscle and sinew in her body seeming to stiffen into immobility. 'I wasn't hiding from you,' she snapped angrily, moving sharply away from him.

Gabe gave her a deeply considering look. 'I didn't say you were hiding from me,' he pointed out softly.

Jane swallowed hard, thinking back to what he had said. No, he hadn't said that exactly, but— 'Or from anyone else, either!' she bit out tautly, glaring at him accusingly.

He shook his head in gentle rebuke. 'You've misunderstood me totally.'

Had she? Minutes ago he had been telling her about Janette Smythe-Roberts, about the fact that she had disappeared three years ago without apparent trace, and now he was asking her how long she'd expected to go on hiding! What conclusion was she supposed to draw from that?

With her own knowledge that she was Janette Smythe-Roberts—his supposed 'perfect' woman he had once seen—there could only be one conclusion to draw. But as Gabe had given no indication, either now or in the past, that he realised she was Janette, perhaps she had jumped to the wrong conclusion...?

She swallowed hard, looking at him with narrowed eyes. 'Kindly explain what you did mean,' she invited stiffly.

He shrugged, a smile playing about those sensuous lips. 'I was referring to your role in the kitchen—always keeping in the background.'

'Always the bridesmaid, never the bride.' She came back with the same comment she had made to her father at the weekend, warning bells still ringing inside her, but a little more quietly now.

'Exactly,' Gabe nodded, grinning openly now. 'While you hide away in other women's kitchens, you're never likely to have one of your own.'

His reply was much like her father's had been too!

'But I already have a kitchen of my own,' she reminded him mockingly. 'You've seen it for yourself.'

'You're being deliberately obtuse now,' he drawled impatiently. 'I meant—'

'I know what you meant, Gabe,' she cut in with dismissive derision. 'And your remarks are presupposing that I want a kitchen of my own.' She shuddered at the thought of it, her experience of marriage definitely not a happy one. 'I'm happy the way I am, Gabe,' she assured him lightly, picking up her evening bag. 'Thank you for the coffee,' she added with finality.

'And goodbye. Again,' he added wryly.

Jane glanced back at him, not unmoved by how ruggedly handsome he was, or that teasing light in his eyes as he looked across at her with raised brows. But he was dangerous—very much so.

'Exactly.' She ruefully acknowledged his last remark. 'That word doesn't seem to have worked too well on you so far!'

'Are you sure you really want it to?' he prompted softly.

'Of course I want it to!' she replied sharply. 'You—'

'Jane, I have a confession to make...' he cut in reluctantly.

She looked at him warily; he already seemed to have said so much tonight! 'Such as?' she challenged brittlely.

He sighed. 'Well, I'm not sure just how close you and Felicity are—'

'I've already told you, I'm not especially close to either of the Warners! I just don't like to see injustice.' She looked at him pointedly.

He gave a mocking inclination of his head. 'Your views were duly noted on that subject,' he drawled self-derisively. 'But I think you should know—just in case Felicity feels duty-bound to mention it at some stage—that I—well, I sort of mentioned to Richard at the weekend that it might be nice if the four of us had dinner together some time!' he admitted, with a pained wince for what her reaction to that was going to be.

Ordinarily she would have been furious at the machinations behind this evening's dinner invitation, but in the circumstances it was difficult to stop herself smiling. There she had been, racking her brain trying to think of some way of seeing him again, albeit so that she could question him about his visit to her parents, and all the time he had been nefariously arranging such a meeting himself!

But Gabe wasn't to know that!

'You really are a man that likes his own way, aren't you?' she said disgustedly. 'So okay, Gabe, we've all had dinner—but I still have to go now,' she added firmly.

'Could we say goodnight rather than goodbye?' he prompted huskily. 'Goodbye is so final, and goodnight leaves a little hope—for me—that we'll meet again.'

Jane couldn't help herself; she did laugh this time, shaking her head ruefully. This man really was impossible.

'Goodnight, Gabe,' she told him dryly.

'There, that wasn't so difficult, was it?' he said with light satisfaction as he walked with her to the door, his arm resting lightly about her shoulders. 'Drive home carefully,' he told her softly.

And, unlike Jane when he had visited her at her apartment last week, Gabe watched her as she walked over to the lift and stepped inside, pressing the button for the ground floor, Gabe still standing in the doorway to his apartment as the lift doors closed.

Gabe had had no need to tell her to drive carefully; she never drove any other way. She was all too aware of how fragile metal and glass could be, the glass smashing, the metal twisting out of all recognition. As fragile as the people inside the vehicle...

She hadn't been the one to go and identify Paul after the accident three years ago; that onerous task had fallen to her father. Jane had been admitted to a private nursing home almost as soon as she'd learnt of the accident, delirious with pain as she lost the baby she had only carried for nine weeks.

It was a time in her life she tried very hard not to think about—Paul's death, his betrayal nothing in comparison with the loss of her baby.

The pregnancy couldn't have happened at a worse time in their marriage: Paul was rarely at home any more, and Jane was no longer bothered by his long absences; in fact she felt relieved by them.

But when she'd found out about the pregnancy she had known that she wanted her baby, wanted it very much, and had thought that perhaps there was something to be salvaged from their marriage after all. But Paul had easily disabused her of that fairy tale, laughingly informing her that he was leaving her to be with Jennifer Vaughan.

Which was what he had been doing at the time of the accident...

The scandal that had followed the two of them being killed together in Paul's BMW had been too much for Jane on top of what she had already suffered. The newspapers had been full of it, her own photograph, as Paul's wife, and that of Gabriel Vaughan, as Jennifer's husband, appearing side by side together in a stream of speculation that had gone on for days on end.

Jane had been too emotionally broken to deal with any of it, and it had been weeks before she was even aware enough to realise that Gabriel Vaughan was looking for her. And as far as she was concerned there had been only one conclusion to draw from his search: somehow he blamed her for the fact that her husband had been involved in an affair with his wife!

That was when she had decided Janette Granger had to disappear, not just for the months she had already been secluded away because of her ill health, but for always if she were ever to make a life for herself.

And so she had disappeared.

But her fear of Gabriel Vaughan had not! Oh, not the Gabe who teased and kissed her; that Gabe was all too easy to like. But the Gabe who had been to visit Daphne and David Smythe-Roberts last week, the Gabe who could still talk so contemptuously of his believed selfishness of Janette Granger; he was definitely a man still to be feared!

And, while Janette Granger might have been able to disappear without apparent trace, Jane Smith knew better than not to heed that fear...

'Good morning, Jane. Lovely morning for a run, isn't it.' Gabe said conversationally as he fell into stride beside her.

Jane faltered only slightly at the unexpected appearance of her running companion, continuing her measured pace.

And Gabe was right about the morning being lovely; it was one of those crisp, clear days so often to be found in England in mid-December, and with the snow now melted it was perfect for her early morning run. Although its perfection had now been marred somewhat by the advent of Gabe at her side! Gabe was the last person she had expected to see running in *her* park at seven o'clock in the morning...!

They ran on in silence, Jane determined not to have her routine disrupted. She enjoyed these early morning runs, putting her brain in neutral, just concentrating on the physical exercise, unhindered by cares or worries.

And this morning was no different as she continued her run round the park. Gabe, at her side, seemed to have no trouble at all keeping pace with her, for all that he must spend most of his time sitting behind a desk.

'I run too when I'm at home.' He seemed to read her thoughts. 'And when I'm not at home I usually find a gym where I can work out.'

She should have known, by the width of his shoulders and the hard muscles of his stomach and legs. 'I'm honoured,' she shot back dryly, looking to neither right nor left as she continued her run.

She didn't believe for a moment that his presence here, at this time, was a coincidence. She had told him last week that she ran in the park near her apartment, and now that he knew the location of that apartment it couldn't have been too difficult for him to work out where it was that she ran. It was the fact that he was here, obviously waiting for her, at seven o'clock in the morning, that had surprised her. And still did.

Gabe glanced sideways noting her concentrated expression. 'I've had some very strange looks while I've been waiting for you!' Again he seemed able to read her thoughts.

Jane could well imagine he had! The only people here at this time of the morning were the homeless who had managed to find—and keep—one of the benches on which to spend the night, and other dedicated runners like herself, exercising before they prepared to go to work. Gabe, in his expensive, obviously new trainers, designer-logo shorts and sweatshirt top, did not fit into either of those categories.

'I'm not surprised,' she drawled, continuing her pounding on the tarmacked pathway.

It was beautiful here at this time of the morning. The birds were singing in the treetops, the sounds of the early morning traffic muted. Ordinarily Jane enjoyed this time of day, but with Gabe for a companion her enjoyment was as muted as the traffic noise!

She stopped once she reached the gate through which she had made her entrance earlier, having worked up a healthy sheen of perspiration, her breasts heaving slightly beneath her white vest-top. Gabe's breathing was much heavier, his chest moving as he took in long gulps of air. Not so untroubled by the exercise as she had assumed!

He looked up at her with a rueful frown. 'Okay, so I haven't managed to find a gym since I arrived two weeks ago; I've been too busy chasing after the most elusive woman I've ever known!' he said irritably as there was no change in her mockingly knowing expression.

Jane stiffened. 'Janette Granger?' she said warily.

'You!' he corrected impatiently. 'Give me a break, Jane. Haven't I proved to you yet that I'm not as ruthless as you initially thought I was?'

Her eyes narrowed, still slightly shaken by his earlier remark. 'Is that what it was all about? Your change of heart where Richard Warner's company was concerned,' she explained scathingly. 'Was it done to impress me?'

Gabe became suddenly still, aqua-blue eyes narrowed angrily. 'You know something, you really are the most—' He broke off abruptly, his mouth a thin, straight line. 'Do you mean to be insulting, Jane, or does it just come naturally to you?' he grated harshly.

She had been thrown by what she had thought was a reference to her past self, and in retrospect she had just been incredibly insulting. After all, it had been three years; she had changed, so why shouldn't he...?

'I'm sorry,' she told him tersely, not quite meeting his own suddenly mocking gaze.

Gabe relaxed slowly, a rueful smile finally curving his lips. 'So what happens now?' He lightly changed the subject. 'Do you go home and take a shower? Or do you have some other form of physical torture—exercise,' he amended dryly, 'in mind first?'

Jane smiled—as she knew she was supposed to do—at his deliberate slip. 'Coffee, croissants, and the newspapers,' she reassured him teasingly.

'Now you're talking!' He lightly grasped her elbow as they turned towards the road. 'I could do with a coffee and a sit down.'

'Oh, we aren't going to sit down yet,' Jane turned to tell him smilingly. 'I pick up the croissants and newspapers, and then I run home for the coffee. Usually,' she added mockingly as she saw his instantly disappointed expression. 'As you've obviously had enough running for one day, I'll make an exception today,' she conceded, leading the way to the little partisserie down one of the side streets away from the park where she usually stopped to buy her croissants on the way home.

As usual the door to the patisserie was already open and the smell of percolating coffee was wafting tempt-ingly out into the street. Several people were already seated at tables as they entered, sipping their coffee, and indulging themselves with the best croissants Jane had ever tasted—her own included.

It wasn't much of a place to look at from the outside, and Jane could see Gabe's eyes widen questioningly as she led the way through the serviceable tables and chairs to the counter beyond.

'Trust me,' she told him softly.

'Without question,' he conceded as softly.

The man behind the counter glanced up from his newspapers as he heard their approach, his handsome face lighting up with pleasure as he saw Jane was his customer. 'Jane, *chérie*,' he greeted in heavily accented English, moving around the counter to kiss her on both cheeks. 'Your usual?' he prompted huskily.

'Usual?' Gabe murmured beside her with dry derision.

She gave him a scathing glance. 'I've brought a friend with me this morning, François.' She spoke warmly to the other man as he looked speculatively at Gabe. 'Two "usuals", to eat in this morning, and two cups of your delicious coffee,' she requested before leading Gabe firmly away to sit at a table by the window.

'First an Italian and now a Frenchman,' Gabe muttered, with a resentful glance towards the handsome François.

Jane looked across the table at him with laughing, sherry-coloured eyes. 'Multinational Jane, that's what they call me!' she returned laughingly. 'Although I'm having more than a little trouble with a certain American I know!'

Gabe returned her gaze with too innocent aqua-blue eyes. 'Me?'

She laughed softly at his disbelieving expression. 'The part of the injured innocent doesn't suit you in the least, Gabe!'

'I—' He broke off as François arrived at their table, expertly carrying the two cups of coffee, two plates containing croissants, and the butter and honey to accompany them. 'That looks wonderful, François.' Gabe spoke lightly to the other man. 'I'm Gabe Vaughan, by the way.' He held out his hand.

François returned the gesture once he had divested himself of the plates and cups. 'Any friend of Jane's is a friend of mine,' he returned a little more coolly.

A coolness that Gabe had obviously picked up on as he gazed speculatively across the table at Jane once the other man had returned to the counter to continue reading his newspaper. 'Exactly how well do—'

'He's a married man, too, Gabe,' she put in curtly. 'Now eat your croissants!' she advised him exasperatedly, already spreading honey on one of her own.

'Yes, ma'am!' he returned tauntingly, turning his attention to the plate of food in front of him.

'At last,' Jane breathed softly seconds later. 'I've found a way to shut you up!' she explained as she watched the expression of first wonder, and then bliss, as it spread across his face after the first mouthful of croissant. As she knew from experience, the pastry would simply melt in his mouth, in an ecstasy of delicacy and taste.

'This guy could make a fortune in the States!' Gabe gasped wonderingly when he could speak again.

'This ''guy'' is doing very nicely exactly where he is, thank you very much,' Jane told him warningly. 'Tempt him away from here at your peril!' She simply couldn't envisage a morning now without François's croissants to start her on her way!

Gabe took another bite of the croissant, as if he couldn't quite believe the first one could have been quite that delicious. 'I'd marry him myself if he weren't already married,' he murmured seconds later. 'How are you on croissants, Jane?' he added, brows arched hopefully.

'Not as good as François,' she answered abruptly. She didn't find any talk of marriage, even jokingly, in the least bit funny!

'Pity,' Gabe shrugged, spreading more honey on what was left of his first croissant. 'I guess I'll just have to stick to François!'

He most certainly would!

Not that she didn't realise he had meant the remark to be a teasing one; it just wasn't a subject she could joke about. And certainly not with Gabriel Vaughan.

Of all people, never with him...!

CHAPTER TEN

'TELL me,' Jane prompted derisively as they lingered over their second cup of coffee, 'what would you have done if I hadn't turned up for a run in the park this morning?' She looked mockingly across at Gabe.

He shrugged. 'I have faith in your determination, Jane, no matter what I may have said to the contrary the other evening!'

She put her cup down slowly, her expression wary. 'My determination...?'

'You don't look in the least like a fair-weather runner to me.' He looked admiringly at her slender figure.

And Jane didn't in the least care for that look.

'After that wonderful meal we had last night, I thought I ought to join you this morning,' he added ruefully. 'I just wasn't sure of your starting time, although I didn't think it would be too late, not with your work schedule,' he added teasingly.

'You're certainly a persistent man,' she said distractedly.

Gabe looked unperturbed. 'Something I inherited from my father—'

'The politician,' Jane recalled dryly.

'Retired,' Gabe acknowledged ruefully, although he looked pleased that she had remembered.

'So he claims.' Jane remembered that conversation only too well. In fact, she remembered all of her conversations with Gabe. 'I usually take a break from running at the weekends,' she explained, still distracted by

132

his persistence . 'It tends to be my busiest time anyway. Although, as it happens, I do usually run later in the morning than this; today I'm up and about early because I'm catering for a lunch.'

'To my good.' He huskily acknowledged the breakfast they had just shared together. 'It would have been even more pleasurable if we hadn't parted at all last night—but I realise I can't have everything!' He looked across at her with teasing eyes.

'You certainly can't where I'm concerned!' Jane dismissed laughingly as she stood up; she had virtually given up trying to stop Gabe coming out with such intimate remarks about the two of them—he took little or no notice of her protests, anyway! 'Time I was going,' she told him briskly. 'I have work to do,' she added pointedly.

'So do I, madam, so do I,' he drawled in rebuke as he followed her back to the counter. 'Let me—'

'My treat,' she insisted firmly, handing over the correct money to François. 'Gabe thinks you should go to the States and make your fortune, François,' she told the other man lightly.

'And deprive myself of the pleasure of paying all these English taxes every year?' François returned with a Gallic shrug. 'Besides, I have an English mother-in-law,' he confided to Gabe with a pointed roll of warm brown eyes. 'And an English mother-in-law has to be the most formidable in the world!' he added heavily.

'All the more reason to leave the country, I would have thought,' Gabe returned sympathetically, his eyes twinkling with his enjoyment of the conversation.

'There is no way she would let me take her two grandchildren with me, let alone her daughter!' François shook his head with certainty. 'Not that my wife would be agreeable to such an idea, either,' he added frowningly. 'You know, ten years ago, when I first met her, she was very sweet and very beautiful, always agreeable. But with the passing of time she grows very like her mother...!' He gave another expressive Gallic shrug.

'Did no one ever warn you to look at the mother before marrying the daughter?' Gabe drawled mockingly.

'Er—excuse me?' Jane cut in pointedly on this man-to-man exchange. Did Gabe get on with everybody? It seemed that he was able to put most people at their ease, was able to adapt to any situation. Strange; three years ago she had had an impression of him being a much more rigid individual... 'When the two of you have quite finished...?' she added ruefully.

Gabe looked down at her with mocking eyes. 'Perhaps it would be a good idea for me to meet your mother...!' he murmured tauntingly.

But he had already done so! And, from the comments he had made to her after that meeting with the Smythe-Robertses, he had obviously liked both her parents.

'Sorry to disappoint you,' Jane derided. 'But I'm nothing like my mother! She's sweet and kind, and has been completely devoted to my father from the day she first met him!' She didn't think she was necessarily unsweet, or unkind, but she had one failed marriage behind her, and no intention of ever repeating the experience!

The two men laughed at her levity, although Gabe's smile faded once they were once again outside in the street, his hand light on her elbow. 'You know, Jane, we can't all be as lucky with our first choice of partner as our parents have been,' he told her gruffly. 'In fact, I've often thought that my own parents' happy marriage gave me the mistaken idea they were all like that!' He shook his head in self-derision.

He could be right in that surmise, Jane allowed. She knew that she had viewed her own marriage, at aged only twenty-one, to be a lifetime commitment to love and happiness. It had taken only a matter of months for her to realise that with Paul that was going to be hard work, if not impossible. But she had made the commitment, and so she had worked at the marriage. Unfortunately, Paul hadn't felt that same need...

'With hindsight, I'm sure our parents' marriages are the exception, not the rule,' she said tightly.

'Probably.' Gabe nodded thoughtfully, glancing at his wristwatch. 'Now that's dinner and breakfast I owe you.' He quirked dark brows. 'Any chance we could start with the dinner?'

And end up having breakfast together the next morning...!

Gabe certainly had to be given marks for trying. After all, he had waited at the park for her this morning in the hope she would turn up. And she hadn't thought that a man like Gabe—rich, handsome, and available—would chase after any woman so persistently, let alone one who was obviously so reluctant to be chased! But perhaps that was the appeal...?

'I did tell you this is my busy time—'

'Even Santa Claus has some time off before the big day,' Gabe reasoned persuasively.

'But as it happens,' she continued firmly, 'I'm free this evening. It's very rare for me to organise a lunch and a dinner on the same day,' she explained dismissively.

'And today you have a lunch,' Gabe said with satisfaction. 'My lucky evening!'

It could be. But then again, it might not be, not if all he was after was a conquest...

'And how do you know Father Christmas takes time off?' she asked inconsequentially.

Gabe burst out laughing. 'I wondered if you would pick me up on that one!'

She would pick him up on anything she felt she should. But as she glanced at him she saw he was looking at his watch once again. 'Am I keeping you from something? Or possibly someone?' she added dryly.

His mouth quirked. 'As it happens—both those things! I have an appointment at ten o'clock, and after our run I need a shower before going to the office.'

Jane's returning smile lacked humour. 'Some other unlucky person whose business is in trouble?'

Gabe shook his head, looking at her with narrowed eyes. 'I would like to know who gave you this detrimental version of my business dealings,' he drawled irritably. 'I could thank them personally!'

Not really! It was Paul who had told her all about Gabriel Vaughan and the way he did business, and he had been out of Gabe's—and anyone else's—reach for three years...

She shrugged. 'It isn't important—'

'Maybe not to you,' Gabe bit out tersely. 'But it sure as hell is to me! I may have stepped in and taken a business over when it was in danger of failing— If I hadn't done it then someone else would have!' he defended harshly at her sceptical expression. 'And at least with me the original workforce, and often the management too, would be kept on if they weren't the reason for the problem.'

As he had with her father's company...except for her father, of course! 'Somehow, Gabe, you don't strike me as a knight in shining armour—'

'I'm well aware of how I strike you, Jane,' he rasped

tautly. 'And I'm doing my damnedest to show you how wrong you are!'

And in part, she realised with a worried frown, he was succeeding. Because several times in their new acquaintance she had been surprised by his actions, found them difficult to place with the ruthless shark she had originally thought him to be...

'Oh, to hell with this,' he suddenly snapped impatiently. 'Just tell me when and where this evening, and I'll meet you there. And try not to make it in yet another establishment where the male proprietor greets you like a long-lost lover, hmm?' he added grimly.

He was jealous! Of Antonio and François. He had been pleasant to both men; in fact, this morning she had noted how easy he found it to get along with people and put them, as well as himself, at their ease. And yet that continued show of relaxation hid another emotion completely.

'Caroline's,' she told him, adding the address of her favourite French restaurant. 'Hopefully we'll be able to get a table for eight o'clock,' she added dryly. 'Although that may be difficult this close to Christmas.'

'Do I take it that Caroline is a female?' Gabe muttered warily.

'You do,' Jane nodded. 'But it's her husband Pierre who does the cooking,' she added with a grin.

'I give up!' Gabe sighed disgustedly, glancing at his watch once again. 'And I'm sure you'll have no trouble getting us a table—even if it is Christmas!' he dismissed exasperatedly. 'I'll meet you there at eight o'clock. Now I really do have to go!' He bent and kissed her briefly on the lips before turning and running off towards the main road where, hopefully, he would be able to flag down a taxi to take him home.

Jane watched him go, ruefully shaking her head as she did so. The man had a way of first bursting in and then bursting out of her life!

And of kissing her whenever he felt like it!

He had dropped that kiss lightly on her lips just now, as if they were two lovers parting briefly to be reunited later in the day. Which was exactly what they were going to do. But they certainly weren't lovers!

Nor ever likely to be either...!

Jane sat at the table waiting, a frown marring her brow as she remembered the telephone message that had been left on her answer machine when she'd got in earlier.

'Janette, darling,' her mother had greeted excitedly. 'Such fun, darling! Daddy and I have decided to come up to London for the day, and we thought it would be marvellous if we could all have tea at the Waldorf like we used to. Daddy and I will be there at four-thirty. But don't worry if you aren't able to make it,' she'd added doubtfully. 'If that's the case I'll give you a ring in a few days' time.'

A few days' time...! There was no way Jane could wait a few days before finding out what had prompted her parents to come up to London.

The London house had been sold three years earlier along with the rest of their surplus needs, and with it most of their London friends had disappeared too. Besides, Jane knew there was little cash to spend on a day in London, let alone tea at the Waldorf...

Tea at the Waldorf had always been a first-day-home-from-boarding-school treat that she and her mother had indulged in, her father usually too busy to join them.

But that wasn't the case today, and luckily Jane had

returned from catering the lunch to receive her mother's recorded message in time for her to get to the Waldorf.

A day in London...

Her parents rarely came to London nowadays, and when they did it wasn't done spontaneously, as this visit appeared to have been. And it was never just for the day; the two of them usually stayed with Jane for several days.

So here she sat, the troubled frown still marring her brow, the time one minute to four-thirty...

Her mother looked transformed as she entered the hotel, radiant in a fine woollen rose-pink suit, her hair newly coloured and styled, her smile graciously lovely as she greeted several other people she knew at the tables as she and Jane's father approached their own reserved table.

Jane's father looked the tall, handsome man she had known when she was a child and teenager, his smiles of greeting as warm as her mother's.

But Jane's feelings of pleasure at the change in her parents were tinged with trepidation as she wondered at the reason for that change...

'Darling!' Her mother kissed her warmly on the cheek as Jane stood up on their arrival at the table.

'Janette.' Her father greeted her more sedately, but there was a teasing glitter in the warmth of his eyes.

'This was a lovely idea,' Jane smiled as they all sat down. 'Thank you both for inviting me.'

But still her feelings of trepidation wouldn't be pushed aside. Although it wouldn't do to just blurt out her curiosity concerning their spontaneity. Besides, she didn't want to wipe out that happy light in the two faces she loved best in the world.

'Have you had an enjoyable day?' she asked casually once their sandwiches and tea had been placed on the table, the latter in front of her mother so that she could pour the Earl Grey into the three china cups. 'It's a little late for Christmas shopping, and the weather hasn't exactly been brilliant for walking around the shops.' There had been flurries of snow and rain most of the day, and the wind was bitterly cold.

'Everywhere looks so festive we didn't notice.' Her mother smiled her pleasure. 'I had forgotten how wonderful everywhere looks at this time of the year,' she added wistfully.

Jane had barely noticed the decorations, she had to admit, not because she didn't like Christmas, but because until the evening of the twenty-fourth of December she would be worked off her feet providing other people's food for the festive season. Christmas Day she would spend with her parents, and on Boxing Day the round of parties and dinners would all begin again. But, yes, everywhere did look rather splendid, and, without her being aware of it until this moment, she was feeling lightened by some of the Christmas spirit herself.

And part of her now wondered just how much of that was due to the presence of Gabriel Vaughan in her life...

She quickly pushed the question to the back of her mind, not wanting to know the answer. He couldn't be coming to mean anything to her; he just couldn't!

'Was there a special reason for your coming up to town today?' she queried as she took her cup of tea from her mother.

Her parents looked briefly at each other before her father answered her. 'Actually, Janette, I had a business meeting. Don't look so surprised.' He laughed at her shocked response to his statement. 'I do still have some contacts in the business world, you know,' he chided teasingly.

And most of those contacts hadn't wanted to know

when he'd run into financial difficulty and had to relinquish his company. To Gabriel Vaughan...

But, whatever had transpired earlier today at this 'business meeting', her father was transformed from that man already grown old at only sixty-one, his shoulders no longer stooped and defeated, that playful twinkle back in his eyes.

'I know you do, Daddy,' she soothed apologetically. 'I just thought—I believed—'

'That I had turned my back on all that,' he finished lightly. 'As most of them turned their back on me,' he added tightly, the first time he—or her mother—had ever indicated the pain they had suffered over the last three years because of the defection of their so-called friends. 'Retirement isn't all it's cracked up to be, you know,' he added wryly, stirring sugar into his tea.

Especially when it had been forced on him!

But, nevertheless, her father was now sixty-one; he couldn't seriously be considering fighting his way back into the business arena at this stage of his life...

Jane looked across at her mother, but her mother only had eyes for her husband: proud and infinitely loving. That love and pride in her mother for her father had never changed.

As it hadn't in Jane. It was just that she could see something else in her mother's gaze today, something she couldn't quite put a name to...

'Well, don't keep me in suspense, Daddy.' She turned back to her father. 'Tell me what you've been up to!'

'I haven't been "up to" anything,' he smiled at her frustration. 'And I'm not sure I should actually tell you anything just yet,' he added less assuredly. 'Not until things are a little more settled. What do you think, Daphne?' A little of the hesitancy that had been with him so much over the last three years crept back into his face as he looked at Jane's mother for guidance.

'I think everything is going to work out splendidly,' Daphne answered him firmly, one of her hands reaching out to rest briefly on his. 'But I'm sure it can all wait until after Christmas,' she added briskly. 'You are still coming to us for Christmas Day, aren't you, Janette?' She looked across at her encouragingly.

Where else could she possibly be going for Christmas? Besides, she always spent Christmas with her parents. Even during the really bad times with Paul, Christmas had been a family time, when they had all been together, happily or not.

And she couldn't say she was particularly happy now with the way the conversation had been turned away from her father's business meeting earlier today. She never had been able to stand mysteries, and that dislike had been heightened during her marriage to Paul, when everything he did and said had become questionable. Until it had got to the stage where she'd stopped asking and he'd stopped telling!

'Of course I am,' she assured them brightly. 'But are you really not going to tell me anything else about what is obviously good news?'

Her father laughed. 'Do you know, Janie, I haven't seen you pout like this since you were a little girl?' he explained affectionately at her hurt look.

Jane gave a rueful grin; maybe she had been trying a little too hard! 'Did it work?' She quirked mischievous brows.

'Maybe back then,' her father conceded warmly. 'But you're twenty-eight now; it doesn't have the same impact.'

She laughed. It was a long time since she had heard

her father being quite this jovial. But she liked it. Whatever the reason for the change in him, and her mother, she could only thank whoever was responsible.

'Drink your tea, Janette,' her mother encouraged briskly. 'Your father and I have a train to catch in a couple of hours.'

She sipped obediently at her tea; her mother was certainly starting to sound like her old self again too. In fact, it felt as if all of them were emerging from a long, dark tunnel...

'Why aren't you staying with me as you usually do?' she prompted lightly. 'Do you have to rush back?'

'You're so busy, darling.' Her mother smiled understandingly. 'We don't want to intrude on what little time you do have for yourself. I know you never mention any young men in your life, but you're so beautiful, darling— more beautiful with your blonde hair, of course,' she sighed, 'but—'

'Now let's not start that, Daphne,' her husband rebuked gently. 'I agree with you, of course, but young women of today seem to change the colour of their hair depending on which outfit they're wearing! Janette may decide to be a flaming redhead by next week!'

'I don't think so, Daddy,' she assured him dryly— although she was glad to have the subject changed from 'young men' in her life! Until Gabe had forced himself into her life just under two weeks ago, there had been no man in her private life at all in the last three years. And she didn't think Gabe was at all the sort of 'young man' her mother was talking about!

'Neither do I, really.' her father gave an answering smile. 'And your mother is right, Janie—you are beautiful. And one bad experience shouldn't sour you for any future—'

'It did, Daddy,' she cut in firmly. 'There have been no young men, there is no young man, and there will be no young men, either!' She didn't consider Gabe a young man at all, and he wasn't in her life—instead he kept trying to pull her into his!

'And just how do you think I'm ever going to become a grandfather if you stick to that decision?' her father chided softly.

'Adoption?' she suggested helpfully.

'Now stop it, you two.' Her mother tutted. 'It's been a wonderful day, it's nearly Christmas, and I won't have the two of you indulging in one of your silly going-nowhere conversations. More tea, David?' she added pointedly.

It was wonderful to see her parents looking, and being, so positive once again. And, Jane realised on her way back to her apartment an hour later, it was the first time for a very long time—three years, in fact!—that she had spent time with her parents without those feelings of guilt that had been like a brick wall between them.

Their lives were changing.

All of them.

Her own because of Gabriel Vaughan, she realised.

But if her parents were to realise, were to know that Gabe was the 'man in her life' at the moment, albeit by his own invitation, how would that affect their own new-found happiness?

Not very well, she accepted frowningly. And nothing, absolutely nothing, must happen to affect her parents' mood of anticipation for the future.

Which meant, she decided firmly, that tonight had to be the last time, the very last time, that she ever saw Gabe...

CHAPTER ELEVEN

'I FIND it very difficult to believe, with the catering connections you seem to have, that you couldn't book a table at a restaurant for us anywhere!' Gabe didn't even pause to say hello as he strolled into her apartment. 'So we're eating at home again, hmm?' He turned in the hallway and grinned at her.

Jane's mouth had dropped open indignantly at his initial bombardment as he came through the open doorway, but his second remark, and that grin—!

'What can I say?' she shrugged. 'It's Christmas!'

Heavens, he looked gorgeous!

She had spent the last two hours telling herself that Gabe meant nothing to her, that they would have dinner together, and then she would tell him this was goodbye. And this time she intended making sure he knew she meant it!

But he did look so handsome in the casual blue shirt worn beneath a grey jacket, and black trousers.

It wasn't true that she couldn't get a table at the restaurant: Caroline and Pierre were old friends; they would have found a table for her even if they'd had to bring another one into the restaurant for her! But a restaurant wasn't the best place for her to say goodbye to him, especially if he should prove difficult—as he had done in the past... And so she had acquired his telephone number from Felicity and called to tell him they were eating at her apartment instead.

'I brought the wine.' Gabe held up a marvellously exclusive—and expensive—bottle of red wine. 'You didn't say what we were eating, but I guessed it wouldn't be beans on toast!' he said with satisfaction.

'You guessed it was eggs, hmm?' she came back derisively.

Gabe gave her a chiding look. 'I've had a good day, Jane; don't spoil it by serving me eggs!'

She grimaced as she took the bottle of wine and went back into the kitchen where she had been when he'd rung the bell. 'Everyone seems to be having a good day today,' she murmured as she uncorked the wine, remembering her parents happiness earlier. 'Stay away from those pots, Gabe,' she warned sharply as he would have lifted one of the saucepan lids. 'Anticipation is half the fun!'

'I know, Jane.'

She became very still, turning slowly to look at him. And then wished she hadn't. Gabe was looking at her as if he would like to make her his main course!

And she'd deliberately dressed down this evening, wearing a green cashmere sweater she had bought several years ago when she was still blonde, and a black fitted skirt, knee-length, not so short as to look inviting.

What she didn't realise was how much more the green colour of her sweater suited the new darkness of her hair, picking out those red highlights—she almost appeared the 'flaming redhead' her father had referred to this afternoon!

'Glasses, Gabe,' she told him through stiff lips.

'Certainly, Jane.' He gave a mocking inclination of his head before strolling across the kitchen, opening the correct cupboard and taking out two glasses.

Maybe having dinner at her apartment wasn't such a good idea, after all! Gabe was too comfortable, too relaxed, altogether too familiar with her home. And not just with her home, either…!

'What shall we drink to?'

While she had been lost in thought, Gabe had poured the wine into the two glasses, holding one out to her now.

'Good days?' he suggested huskily.

That had to be better than 'us'!

This had not been a good idea. She could only hope the time would pass quickly.

'Why don't you go through to the sitting-room and pick out some music to play while I serve our first course?' she suggested abruptly, her usual calm having momentarily deserted her.

But then, when didn't it when she was around this man? It was past time to say goodbye to him!

'So why did you have a good day?' she prompted conversationally as they sat down to their garlic prawns with fresh mayonnaise, an old John Denver CD of hers playing softly in the background.

Gabe's gaze met hers laughingly. 'Well, this morning I went for a run for the first time in two weeks—'

'Shame on you, Gabe!'

'Mmm, this tastes wonderful, Jane.' He had just tasted his first prawn dipped in the mayonnaise. 'I can hardly wait to see what we have for the main course!'

With any luck, his enjoyment of the food would stop him talking too much.

She could live in hope!

The wine, as she had already guessed when she'd seen the label, was beautiful—rich and silky smooth. Only the best for Gabriel Vaughan.

'Did you have a good day too?' Gabe looked up from his food to ask her, frowning at her derisive smile. 'What…?' he prompted warily.

She gave a mocking shake of her head. 'We don't have to play those sorts of games, Gabe,' she told him dryly. 'We're having dinner, not spending the rest of our lives together!' she explained scornfully at his puzzled expression.

'It starts with conversation, Jane, eating dinner together, finding out about each other, likes and dislikes, things like that. People don't leap straight into marriage—'

'I don't believe I mentioned the word marriage, Gabe.' She stood up abruptly, their first course at an end as far as she was concerned.

'As I've already said,' Gabe murmured, turning in his chair to watch her departure into the kitchen, 'he must have been some bastard.'

She didn't remember him saying any such thing! But, nevertheless, he was right; that was exactly what Paul had been.

Their used plates landed with a clatter on the kitchen worktop, her hands shaking so badly she'd had trouble carrying them at all.

What was wrong with her?

She had made a conscious decision this afternoon to tell Gabe this was definitely the last time they would see each other. One look at him and she knew her resolve had weakened. One smile from him, and she began to tremble. If he should actually touch her—

'Anything wrong—? Hell, Jane, I only touched your arm!' Gabe frowned down at her darkly as Jane had literally jumped away from the touch of his hand on her arm. 'What the hell is wrong with you tonight?'

She had asked herself the same question only seconds ago!

And, looking at him, she was beginning to realise what the answer was...

No!

She couldn't have those sorts of feelings towards Gabe, couldn't actually want him to touch her, to make love to her?

But she did; she knew she did! And she hadn't felt this way since— But no—she hadn't ever felt quite this way towards Paul. She'd never trembled at the thought of him touching her, had never ached for his lips on hers.

But she'd loved Paul. She wasn't in love with Gabe. If she was anything, she was in lust with him!

Oh, God...!

'What is it, Jane?' he prompted again, his frown having deepened to a scowl at her continued silence.

She had to pull herself together, finish the meal—she doubted he would consider leaving before then!—and then she must make it absolutely plain to him that she did not want him appearing in her life whenever he felt like it; that there would be no more runs together in the park, no more turning up at her apartment, and no more impatient messages left on her answer machine.

And, most important of all, there would be no further occasion for him to kiss her!

'Sorry,' she dismissed lightly. 'My thoughts were miles away when you came into the kitchen, and I'm a little tired too, I'm afraid.' She gave him a bright, meaningless smile as she voiced these excuses for her extraordinary behaviour, at the same time totally distancing herself from him as she crossed the kitchen to check on the food simmering on the hob. 'If you would like to go back to the dining area, I'll serve our main course and bring it through in a few minutes.'

She deliberately didn't look up at him again before she

began to do exactly that, but all the time she busied herself with the food she was aware of him still standing across the other side of the kitchen, watching her with narrowed, puzzled eyes. And then, with a frustrated shake of his head, he turned and impatiently left the room.

Jane leant weakly against the table in the middle of the kitchen. She had never wanted any man the way she wanted Gabe!

And there was no way, simply no way, she could ever assuage this sudden hunger she felt for his kisses and his touch.

She had always thought of him—when she'd allowed herself to think of him at all—as a man who took his pleasure where he found it, and then moved on. But the one thing she had learnt about him since his reappearance into her life was that if Gabe wanted something, then he didn't relinquish his right to it easily. And she didn't doubt for a moment that, physically at least, Gabe wanted her as much as she wanted him.

And she also didn't doubt that to give him what he wanted wouldn't mean it would end there...

Goodbye was the word she had to say to him. Not angrily; it had to be said in such a way that he would never want to come back.

The ache inside her would go away, she assured herself as she served the noisettes of lamb with tarragon sauce and the still crunchy vegetables from the steamer, and then everything could go back to the way she liked it—untroubled, and uncomplicated.

Why did that realisation suddenly hold no appeal for her?

Ridiculous. That was what this whole situation was—ridiculous! Thank you. And goodbye. Four words. Very easy to say.

But could she say them as if she meant them?

Her heart skipped a beat when Gabe turned to smile at her as she came in with the food.

Thank you. And goodbye, she repeated firmly to herself. She would say them. And mean them!

'Cooking dinner for us this evening has been too much for you,' Gabe told her apologetically as she sat down opposite him. 'I should have thought of that when you telephoned me earlier. You've already been at work today; the last thing you needed this evening was to cook another meal.' He shook his head self-disgustedly. 'The least I could have done was offer to cook for you.' He sighed ruefully.

Jane knew from watching him the other evening that he was more than capable of doing it, too. But spend the evening at his apartment...? She didn't think so!

'Don't give it another thought, Gabe,' she dismissed— knowing that he'd been thinking about it ever since he'd left the kitchen a few minutes ago. And the reason he had come up with for her skittishness was obviously that she had been working too hard. 'Cooking for two people, and in the comfort of my own home, isn't work at all,' she assured him.

'But the whole point of this evening was that I would take you out,' he protested.

'You know, Gabe,' she said softly, 'I'm one of those chefs that's inclined to turn nasty if my food isn't eaten while it's still hot!'.

He seemed on the point of protesting again for several seconds, and then he grinned, relaxing once again as he picked up his knife and fork in preparation for eating. 'Never let it be said...!'

Jane ate sparingly, her appetite having deserted her

with the realisation that after a couple of hours' time she would never see this man again.

How had he crept into her emotions like this—even lustful ones? *When* had he?

'—parents arrive in the country tomorrow, and I wondered if you could join us all for dinner tomorrow evening?'

Jane blinked across at him, having been lost in her own thoughts, and slowly took in what he had just said to her. His parents were arriving in London tomorrow? And why not? It was Christmas, and, from what he had said, he was an only child, too. But as for the suggestion of her having dinner with them...!

'I've told you, Gabe,' she replied lightly. 'This is my busy time of year. I'm catering for a party of thirty people tomorrow evening,' she said thankfully.

'You work too damned hard,' he bit out disapprovingly.

'I like to eat myself occasionally.' She wryly pointed out the necessity for her to work. Maybe Gabe had forgotten what that was like; he was certainly in a financial position not to have to work any more, but she certainly wasn't!

He scowled heavily. 'You shouldn't have to—'

'Now, now, Gabe,' she cut in tauntingly. 'Don't let your chauvinism show!'

'This isn't funny, Jane.' He frowned across at her. 'When I think—'

'I often think that the mere act of thinking only complicates things at times,' she dismissed calmly, putting down her knife and fork, the food only half eaten on her plate, although Gabe seemed to have enjoyed his, his plate now empty. 'Would you like your cheese or dessert next? People seem to vary in their preference nowadays, I've noticed.'

'Actually—' he sat forward, leaning his elbows on the table as he looked straight at her '—I'd like an answer to my original question.'

She raised dark brows. 'Which question was that, Gabe?' But she knew which one it was. She also knew that she had no intention of meeting his parents, now or ever! After this evening she wouldn't be seeing him again, either...

His mouth quirked, and he gave a slight shake of his head. 'It isn't going to work this time, Jane. I would very much like you to meet my parents,' he told her bluntly. 'And for them to meet you.'

'Why?' she came back just as bluntly.

'Because they're nice people.' he shrugged.

His parents wouldn't be the ones under inspection at such a meeting; she would. And she had been through all this once before in her life, eight years ago. She'd tried so hard at the time to win the approval of Paul's parents, little knowing that she needn't have bothered. The fact that she was the only child of very rich parents was the only asset she had needed in the eyes of Paul's parents! It had never occurred to the elder Grangers that money could be lost more easily than it had been made...

Jane hadn't seen or heard from Paul's parents since just before Paul's death. On the one occasion she had attempted to telephone them they had claimed they would never forgive her for not even being at their son's funeral. The fact that she had been in a clinic at the time, having just lost her baby—their own grandchild—and that Paul had been in the company of another woman at the time of his accident, hadn't seemed to occur to them...

'Do you introduce all your friends to them, Gabe?' The derision could be heard in her voice.

He didn't even blink, his gaze remaining steady on hers. 'The ones that matter, yes!'

She gave a humourless smile. 'We barely know each other, Gabe. Did you introduce Jennifer to them before you married her?' she couldn't resist adding.

And then wished she hadn't! Jennifer had been his wife; their own relationship wasn't in the same category.

'As it happens, yes, I did.' He relaxed back in his chair, smiling lazily. 'My father was bowled over by the way she looked; my mother hated her on sight.' He gave a wry chuckle. 'I'm sure I don't have to tell you which one proved to be right!'

From what Jane knew of Jennifer Vaughan, men had always been 'bowled over' by the way she looked. And the majority of women seemed to have disliked her intensely. Herself included.

'That can't have been easy for you,' Jane sympathised.

'Nothing about that relationship was easy for me,' he acknowledged grimly. 'And you're changing the subject again, Jane—'

'Because I don't want to meet your parents, Gabe,' she sighed, becoming impatient with his persistence.

'Why not?' he came back as bluntly as she had minutes ago.

'Several reasons—'

'Name them,' he put in forcefully, no longer relaxed, sitting upright in his chair, his gaze narrowed on her.

'I was about to,' she rebuked softly; she did not want to get into an argument about this; she disliked arguments intensely. There had been too many of them with Paul. 'Firstly, it puts a completely erroneous light on our friendship.' She deliberately used the casual term, knowing he had registered that fact by the way his mouth tightened ominously. 'And secondly,' she added less confidently, knowing she was going to have that argument whether she wanted it or not, 'I don't think the two of us should see each other again after tonight!' It all came out in a rush, so desperate was she to get it over with as quickly as possible.

Gabe raised those expressive dark brows. 'And exactly what brought this on?' he questioned mildly.

'Nothing "brought this on", Gabe,' she returned exasperatedly. 'I've been telling you to go away, one way or another, since the night we first met!' For all the good it had done her!

'Exactly,' he nodded. 'But this time you seem to mean it...' he said thoughtfully.

'I meant it all the other times too!' Jane claimed scathingly, wondering, in the light of the fact that she had now, inwardly at least, acknowledged her attraction towards him, whether she *had* really meant all those other refusals she had given him...

'Did you?' Gabe seemed to doubt it too!

Of course she had meant them, she told herself strongly. Gabriel Vaughan was a man for her to avoid, not encourage. Besides, she was sure she hadn't encouraged him. Not consciously, at least...

But subconsciously? Had she been forceful enough in telling him to go away? She had thought so at the time. But—

Enough of this! It was just confusing her.

She stood up abruptly, intending to clear their plates. And there would be no cheese or dessert. After this conversation, a little earlier in the meal than she had anticipated, she acknowledged, it was time for Gabe to leave!

'I meant it, Gabe,' she told him forcefully. 'I don't

want to have dinner with you. I don't want to meet your parents. And, most important of all, I don't want to see you again! There, I can't be any plainer than that.' She looked down at him with challenging brown eyes.

He coolly returned her furious gaze. 'And what about the Christmas present I got for you today?' he said softly.

Present? He had bought her a Christmas present? 'I think you were a little premature in buying me anything!' she told him impatiently. 'But with any luck you'll have found someone else before Christmas that you can give it to instead—after all, there are still a few days to go!'

'Hmm, so we're back to the insults, are we?' Gabe murmured thoughtfully as he stood up. 'The present was meant for you, Jane, not someone else,' he bit out harshly, reaching out to clasp her arms.

Jane suddenly had trouble breathing, knowing it was due to Gabe's close proximity. 'I don't—'

'Want it,' he completed harshly. 'You know, Jane, determination, and a certain independence of spirit, is to be admired in a woman. But not,' he added dismissively as she would have made an angry reply, 'when they are taken to the extreme of pigheaded rudeness! You went past that point several minutes ago,' he added tightly.

'I—'

'Shut up, Jane,' he rasped, pulling her effortlessly towards him.

'You can't—'

'Please!' he added with a groan, his head bending and his lips claiming hers.

Jane melted.

It was as if she had been waiting for this moment since he had kissed her so lightly this morning. And there was nothing light or distracted about this kiss; all Gabe's attention was focused on the passion that flared up between thcm so easily. Like tinder awaiting the flame. And it seemed they were that flame for each other...

Her arms moved up about his neck, one hand clinging to the broad width of his shoulder, the other becoming entangled in the dark thickness of his hair, her body held tightly against his, moulded to each muscle and sinew.

Without removing his lips from hers Gabe swung her up into his arms and carried her over to the soft gold-coloured sofa, laying her down on it before joining her there, their bodies even closer now, their breath mingling, Gabe's hands moving restlessly over the slenderness of her back and thighs.

Jane gasped softly as one of those hands moved to cup her breast, the gently sloping curve fitting perfectly against his own flesh, the nipple responding instantly to the gentle caress of his thumb, the tip hardening to his touch, a pleasurable warmth spreading through her thighs all the way to the tips of her toes.

She wanted this man!

Not like this, with their clothes between them, she wanted the naked warmth of his body next to hers, wanted to feel his hard possession, wanted to give him the same pleasure he was undoubtedly giving her.

His hand was beneath the woollen cashmere of her jumper now, and he was groaning low in his throat at his discovery that she wasn't wearing a bra, her breast naked to his touch.

Her breasts had always been firm and uplifting, definitely one of her better assets, and she rarely saw the necessity to wear a bra.

She groaned low in her own throat now as Gabe pushed aside the woollen garment, his head bending as his lips claimed possession of that fiery tip, his tongue rasping with slow, moist pleasure across her sensitive flesh.

She was on fire, offered no protest when, hindered by its presence, Gabe pulled the jumper up over her head and discarded it completely. Her gaze was shy as she looked up at him and he looked at her with such pleasurable intensity.

'You're beautiful, Jane,' he murmured huskily. 'But then, I always knew you would be!' he groaned before his head lowered, his mouth capturing hers with fierce intensity, passion flaring uncontrollably now, carrying them both on a tide that was going to be impossible to stop.

Not that Jane had any thought of bringing this to an end. She wanted Gabe as badly as he appeared to want her. She had never known such need, such desire, trembling with anticipation, knowing—

'Oh, Janie, Janie!' Gabe groaned as he buried his face in the warmth of her neck, breathing in deeply of her perfume. 'If you only knew how I've wanted this, how long I've needed to hold and kiss you like this.' His arms tightened about her as his lips travelled the length of her throat.

Jane felt cold. Icy.

Janie...

He had called her *Janie*. Only her father had ever called her by that pet name.

It could be coincidence, of course, Gabe's own arousal making him unaware of what he had just said.

Or just carelessness...?

Gabe tensed beside her, suddenly seeming to become aware of the way she had moved as far away from him as she was able on the confines of the sofa, slowly lifting his head so that he could look down at her, his expression—wary!

She wasn't mistaken.

It wasn't coincidence!

She moistened suddenly dry lips. 'How long, Gabe?' she demanded coldly.

He frowned. 'How long...?' he repeated, that wariness having increased.

She nodded, more certain with every second that passed that she wasn't mistaken in the conclusion she had just come to. 'How long have you known exactly who I am?' she said plainly.

Because he did know.

She was sure now that he did.

So why hadn't he told her that days ago...?

CHAPTER TWELVE

'How long have you known, Gabe?' she repeated in a steady voice, fully clothed again now, standing across the room looking over to where Gabe still sat on the couch.

He drew in a ragged breath, running agitated fingers through the darkness of his hair. 'I—'

'Don't even attempt to avoid answering me, Gabe,' she warned harshly. 'We both know—now—that you realise I was once Janette Smythe-Roberts!'

How long had he known? she asked herself again. And why hadn't he said so as soon as he made the discovery?

She literally went cold at the only explanation she could think of!

'You still are Janette Smythe-Roberts, damn it!' he rasped, standing up himself now, instantly dwarfing what had already seemed to her to be a space too small to hold them both.

She felt sick, had perhaps cherished some small hope inside her that he really didn't know. But his words confirmed that he did!

'Don't come near me.' Jane cringed away from him as he would have reached out and touched her. 'You still haven't told me exactly how long you've known,' she prompted woodenly.

Or what he was going to do about it! He hadn't been behaving like a man still out to wreak vengeance, but perhaps making her want him was his way of exacting retribution…?

Gabe gave a weary sigh, shrugging wide shoulders. 'I

160

realised who you were about thirty seconds after I came into the kitchen with Felicity last week,' he admitted quietly.

Jane drew in a shaky breath, her arms wrapped about herself protectively. 'That long? How on earth—?'

'Your hair may be a different colour, Jane,' he rasped. 'And your face has taken on a certain maturity it didn't once have. But it's still the same face I remember,' he added huskily. 'A face I'll never forget.'

She shook her head disbelievingly. 'But I never even saw you face to face until last week—'

'But I saw you,' Gabe cut in firmly. 'We were never actually introduced to each other, but I saw you at a party one evening with your husband.'

Her husband. Gabe's wife's lover. The man Jennifer had left him for.

She sighed. 'I don't remember that evening.' She shook her head; a lot of the time before the accident was a blank to her, her misery as Paul's wife already well established.

'You looked beautiful that night,' Gabe recalled softly. 'You were wearing a brown dress, the same colour as your eyes, little make-up that I could see—but then, you don't need make-up to enhance your beauty. And your hair—! I had never seen hair quite that colour before, or that long; it reached down to your waist like a curtain of gold! I didn't need to be introduced to you to remember you, Jane—you stood out in that crowd like a golden light in darkness!'

Her mouth twisted scornfully. 'Please stop waxing lyrical about me, Gabe; I was very unhappy at that time; I probably didn't even want to be there. I no longer loved my husband but felt trapped in the marriage—'

'Until he walked out of it!'

'Until Paul walked out of it,' she acknowledged shakily. 'To be with your wife,' she added hardly.

Gabe shrugged. 'So the fairy story goes,' he said dryly.

Jane gave him a sharp look. 'There was no fairy-tale ending to that particular story—for any of us! And you've been playing with me for the last twelve days—'

'To what end?' he challenged harshly.

'I have no idea.' She sighed wearily. 'I presume for the same reason you tried to find me after the accident.' She shrugged.

'The same reason. But not the one you think! And I backed off then when I heard the rumour that you had lost your baby,' he rasped.

'Did you?' she said heavily, no longer looking at him but staring sightlessly at her music centre. The CD had long since finished playing. But neither of them had noticed that fact; they'd been too engrossed in each other at the time. Which brought her back to Gabe's kisses and caresses. Was he still trying to make someone pay for what happened three years ago? 'Then you know that if anyone was a victim of my husband's relationship with your wife, Gabe,' she bit out evenly, 'it was my unborn baby!'

'Jane—'

'I told you not to come near me!' she flared as he made a move towards her, her eyes flashing in warning. 'What did you think when you met me again last week, Gabe?' She looked at him challengingly. 'Did you see I had nothing left to lose and decide to hurt me in another way?'

He became suddenly still. 'What way?'

'You tell me!' She smiled humourlessly. 'Those conversations we had about Janette Smythe-Roberts.' She shook her head disgustedly. 'You were playing with me all the time!' she realised self-derisively. And all the time she had thought she was the one not being completely honest!

'I was trying to get you to defend yourself!' Gabe returned impatiently. 'But you didn't do it,' he added disappointedly.

'Didn't defend myself against being thought a cold-blooded, manipulative gold-digger? Someone who would take money from my parents and leave them almost penniless?' Jane looked at him scathingly. 'As I told you once before, Gabe, you sweep through people's lives, uncaring of the chaos and pain you leave behind you—'

'That isn't true!' His hands were clenched angrily.

'Perhaps uncaring is the wrong word to use,' she conceded disgustedly. 'You're simply unaware of it! Which is perhaps even worse. What do you think happens to people when you've stepped in and bought their company, possibly their life's work, out from under them? Do you think they simply shrug their shoulders and start all over again?' she challenged.

'It's business, Jane—'

'So my father said when he tried to explain your behaviour to me!' she scorned. 'But I call it something else completely!'

Gabe drew in a harsh breath. 'Let's not lose sight of the real villain here, Jane,' he rasped. 'And it wasn't me!'

Paul... It always came back to Paul. And with thoughts of Paul came ones of Gabe's wife Jennifer...

'If you're going to blame Paul for this then let's include your wife in it too,' Jane said with distaste. 'Who do you think he was trying to impress with his gambling and high living?'

Gabe became suddenly still. 'I accept Jennifer's blame—'

'Do you?' Jane gave another mirthless smile. 'She was beautiful, immoral, utterly uncaring of anyone but herself. She knew of my pregnancy, too, because Paul had told her, but it made no difference when she decided she wanted my husband—'

'Jennifer couldn't have children herself,' Gabe put in softly. 'She'd had tests. She was infertile. Pregnant women represented a threat to her.'

Jane felt the momentary sadness that she would for any woman unable to have children of her own. But it was only momentary where Jennifer Vaughan was concerned. 'That didn't give her the right to entice away the husbands of those women!'

'I agree.' Gabe sighed heavily. 'But it's an inescapable fact that that's exactly what she did. With dire results in your particular case.'

Jane stared at him as she fully registered all that he had just said. 'Are you telling me that that wasn't the first time Jennifer had done something like that?' It seemed incredible, but that was exactly what it sounded like he was saying!

He ran a weary hand across his brow. 'Jennifer was a very troubled woman. The fact that she couldn't have children—'

'I asked you a question, Gabe,' Jane cut in tautly.

He looked at her steadily. 'I believe I've already told you that Jennifer was much more interested in other women's husbands than she was in her own—'

'But pregnant women in particular?' Jane persisted.

'Yes!' he acknowledged harshly, turning away. 'To Jennifer there was nothing more beautiful than a pregnant woman. To her they seemed to glow. More importantly, they carried life inside them. A pregnant woman became the ultimate in beauty to her.'

'That's ridiculous!' Jane snapped. 'Most pregnant women don't feel that way at all. Oh, there's a certain magic in creating life, in feeling that life growing inside you,' she remembered emotionally. 'But for the most part you feel nauseous, and in the beginning it's a nausea that never seems to stop. And, added to that, you feel fat and unattractive—'

'Pregnant women aren't fat,' Gabe cut in softly. 'They're blossoming.'

'That's a word only used by people who aren't pregnant,' Jane put in dismissively. 'Believe me, most of us just feel fat!' And that feeling hadn't been helped, in her case, by the fact that Paul had obviously found her condition most unattractive!

'Maybe,' Gabe conceded with a sigh. 'But to a woman who has never been pregnant, and who never can be, that isn't how pregnancy appears at all. Oh, I'm not excusing Jennifer's behaviour—'

'I hope not,' Jane told him tightly. 'Because it isn't a good enough excuse as far as I'm concerned!' She had lost her baby—the only good thing to come out of her marriage—because her husband had left her for Jennifer Vaughan, and the two of them had subsequently died together in a car crash. There was no excuse for that!

'It isn't a good enough excuse for any woman,' Gabe accepted heavily. 'But it's what Jennifer did.'

'Then why didn't you leave her?' Jane frowned. 'Why did you stay with her, and in doing so condone her behaviour?'

A nerve pulsed in his tightly clenched jaw. 'I didn't condone it, Jane. I would never condone such behaviour. But I thought that by staying with her I could—' He shook his head. 'I don't believe in divorce, Jane,' he told her abruptly. 'And neither did Jennifer,' he added softly.

She became suddenly still, her frown deepening. Jennifer didn't believe in divorce…? 'But she left you…'

Gabe sighed. 'No. She didn't.'

'But—'

'I know that's what Paul told you three years ago, and it's what everyone else thought at the time too, but I can assure you, Jennifer was not leaving me.' He shook his head. 'There were so many times I wished she would,' he admitted harshly. 'But I was her safety net, the let-out when any of her little affairs became too serious. As Paul did…'

Jane was having trouble absorbing all of this now. Was Gabe really saying what she thought he was?

Paul had said he was leaving her, that he and Jennifer were going to be together.

'Are you telling me—?' She ran her tongue over suddenly dry lips. 'Are you saying that Paul and Jennifer weren't going away together?'

'That's exactly what I'm saying.' Gabe nodded grimly. 'Jennifer was furious the day of the accident. Paul had telephoned her to say he'd left you, and now he expected her to do the same to me. She met him that day only so that she could tell him what a fool he was, that she had no intention of leaving me, that he had better hurry home and make it up with his wife before she decided his leaving had been the best thing that ever happened to her! Her words, Jane, not mine,' Gabe told her bleakly.

But it had already been too late for Paul to do that. She might not already have realised that Paul's leaving 'had been the best thing that ever happened to her', but Paul had been in too deeply in other ways to backtrack on his decision. As her father's assistant, he had stolen money from the company, and in doing so had brought that company almost to the point of ruin.

'I've often wondered if it was an accident,' Gabe murmured softly, as if partly reading her thoughts.

Jane looked at him dazedly. Not an accident? What was he saying, suggesting? But hadn't she just told herself there had been no way back for Paul, that he had already burnt his bridges, both professionally and privately? But could he have thought that there was no reason to carry on? No, she wouldn't believe that! Paul had been too selfish, too self-motivated, to take his own and Jennifer's lives.

'It's something we'll never know the answer to,' Gabe continued gently. 'Probably something best not known.'

Jane agreed with him. That sort of soul-searching could do neither of them any good. No matter what the reason for doing so…

'Love is a very strange emotion,' she said dully. 'It appears to grow and exist for people who really don't deserve it.' And Jennifer Vaughan certainly hadn't deserved Gabe's, or any other man's, love. And yet who but a man in love could ever have thought her the 'perfection' he had once called her?

'Death is rather final,' Gabe muttered. 'But you're still well rid of Paul Granger!'

'I've never—' She shook her head. 'We're getting away from the point here—'

'Maybe I caught that from you.' Gabe attempted to tease, although he couldn't even bring himself to smile, let alone encourage her to do so. 'What is the point here, Jane? You tell me.' He shook his head. 'Because I've certainly lost it!'

For the main part, so had she! Except that Gabe had known exactly who she was for the last twelve days. And for reasons of his own he had chosen to keep that fact to himself!

She looked at him coldly. 'The point is that for me the past is as dead and buried as Paul himself is. Why do you think I've been asking you to go away for the last twelve days? Because you remind me of a time I would rather forget,' she told him bluntly.

Gabe looked pale now. 'I didn't imagine what happened between us a short time ago—'

'It's been a long time for me, Gabe,' she said scornfully. 'My marriage may have been a mistake, but despite all that I'm still a normal woman, with normal desires, and you—'

'Just happened to be here!' he finished disgustedly. 'Is that it, Jane?'

No, that wasn't it! She had met plenty of other men over the last three years, much more suitable men, men just as handsome as he was, just as interested in a relationship with her. And she hadn't responded to any of them, hadn't allowed any of them as close to her as this man had got in a matter of days.

But to find the reason for that she would have to delve into her own emotions. And she had already done enough of that where Gabriel Vaughan was concerned.

'That just about sums it up, yes!' she confirmed hardly. 'It probably has something to do with the time of year, too,' she added insultingly. 'Let's face it, no one likes to be on their own at Christmas!'

And strangely, despite the fact that this Christmas was actually going to be no different from the last three she had spent with her parents, she had a feeling she was going to feel very much alone...

What had Gabe done to her? What was it that she felt towards him? Because it was no longer that mixture of fear and apprehension she had felt before .

Gabe gave a pained wince at her deliberate bluntness.

'I had better make myself scarce, then, hadn't I?' He picked up his jacket, but didn't put it on. 'That way you still have time to meet someone else before the big day!'

Although his words hurt—as they were meant to do!—Jane offered no defence. Nor did she try to stop him as he walked out of the door, closing it softly behind him.

There would have been no point in stopping him. They had said all that needed to be said. Probably more than needed to be said!

And she still had no idea why Gabe had pursued her so relentlessly for the last twelve days. She felt he had offered no real explanation for such extraordinary behaviour when he had known all the time she was Janette Smythe-Roberts.

Two things she did know only too clearly, though.

One; Gabe must have loved his wife very much; he must have done to have tolerated her behaviour. Secondly—and this was against all that she had tried to do for herself for the last three years—she didn't need to delve into her own emotions to find out why she had responded to Gabe in the way that she had. She had known the answer to that question as soon as he had closed the door behind him...

Somehow—and she wasn't sure how such a thing could have happened—she had fallen in love with Gabe!

Stupidly.

Irrevocably!

CHAPTER THIRTEEN

JANE made the drive to her parents' home on Christmas morning with more than her usual reluctance. The last few days, since Gabe had walked out of her life for good, had been such a strain to get through, and as a consequence she looked paler than usual, despite the application of blusher.

And even in those few days she had lost enough weight for it to be noticeable. She had put on a baggy thigh-length jumper, burnt orange in colour, and styled black trousers, in an effort to hide this fact from her parents. But there was nothing she could do to hide the gauntness of her face, or the dull pain in her eyes that wouldn't go away.

She had let Gabriel Vaughan get to her. Not only that, she had allowed herself to fall in love with him.

Maybe that was what he had hoped for, she had told herself over and over again in the last few days, when not even her work could blot him from her mind and senses. If it was, then he had succeeded, even if he wasn't aware of it.

At least, she hoped he wasn't aware of it. That would be the ultimate pain in this whole sorry business!

Jane drew in a deep breath after parking her van, forcing a bright smile to her lips as she got out and walked towards the house. It was only a few hours of forced gaiety; surely she could handle that? After all, it was Christmas Day!

'You're looking very pale, darling,' her mother said,

sounding concerned, kissing her in greeting as she did so.

'And you've lost weight, too,' her father added reprovingly after giving her a hug.

So much for her efforts at camouflage!

'You're both looking well too,' she returned teasingly. 'And one of your Christmas lunches, Mummy, should take care of both those things!' she assured them lightly.

'I hope so,' her father said sternly. 'But first things first—a glass of my Christmas punch?'

'Guaranteed to put us all to sleep this afternoon!' Jane laughed, finding she was, after all, glad to be home with her parents on this special day.

'I sincerely hope not.' Her mother smiled. 'We have guests arriving after lunch!'

It was the first Jane had heard of anyone joining them on Christmas Day, but even if company was the last thing she felt in need of she was glad for her parents' sake. Whatever it was her father had become involved with on a business level, it had obviously given their social life a jolt too; it was years since they had spent Christmas with the house full of people.

Besides, company would take the pressure off her.

'In that case, I suggest we drink our punch and open our presents.' She had brought her parents' presents with her. 'And then I can help you cook lunch, Mummy,' she offered—Mrs Weaver always spent Christmas with her sister in Brighton. 'Windy, cold place this time of year', the housekeeper invariably complained, but Jane's parents insisted she must be with her family at Christmastime.

'Busman's holiday, Janie?' her father teased.

Her smile wavered for only a fraction of a second. The last person to call her Janie had been Gabe. No, she wouldn't think of him any more today! Her parents were in very good spirits, and she would allow none of her own unhappiness to spill over and ruin their day for them.

Which proved more than a little difficult later that afternoon when the 'guests' turned out to be Gabe and his parents!

It hadn't even occurred to Jane to ask who the guests were going to be, having assumed it was friends of her parents whom she had known herself since childhood, friends she could feel perfectly relaxed with.

A tall, handsome man, dark hair showing grey at his temples, entered the room first with her mother, her parents having gone together to answer the ring of the doorbell. Her father entered the room seconds later with a tall, blonde-haired woman, elegantly beautiful, her soft American drawl as she spoke softly sending warning bells through Jane even before Gabe entered the room behind the foursome.

Jane was dumbstruck. Never in her worst nightmare could she have imagined her parents inviting Gabe and his parents here on Christmas Day! They barely knew Gabe, let alone his parents, so why on earth—?

But even as she stared disbelievingly across at Gabe, his own gaze coolly challenging as he met hers, Jane knew exactly what Gabe and his parents were doing here. That day, when her mother and father had come to London so unexpectedly, had also been the day Gabe had told her he had an important business meeting he had to get to for ten o'clock...!

Gabe was the person who had offered her father some sort of business opening, was the reason why her father looked so much younger, and her mother looked so much more buoyant!

He couldn't! He couldn't be going to hurt her parents

all over again? He—

No, she answered herself confidently even as the idea came into her head. The man she had come to know over the last two weeks, the man she loved, wouldn't do that Then why? What was it all about? What did it all mean?

'Think about it a while, Jane.' Gabe had strolled casually across the room to stand at her side, his tone pleasant, but those aqua-blue eyes were as cold as ice.

Like the blue of an iceberg Jane had once seen in a photograph...

'Really think about it, Jane,' he muttered harshly. 'But in the meantime come and say hello to my parents.'

The trouble was, she couldn't think at all; she wasn't even aware that she was being introduced to his father, although she did note that he was an older version of his son, the only difference being that on the older man the aqua-blue eyes were warm and friendly as he shook her hand.

Marisa Vaughn, although aged in her early sixties, was undoubtedly a beautiful woman, possessed of an air of complete satisfaction with her life.

Jane found she couldn't help but like and feel drawn to both the older Vaughns.

'Janette is such a pretty name,' Marisa Vaughn murmured huskily. 'It suits you, my dear.' She squeezed Jane's arm warmly before turning away to accept the glass of punch being poured to warm them all.

'Janette has just suggested the two of us go for a walk,' Gabe put in loudly enough that the four older people could hear him over their own murmur of conversation. 'Would any of you care to join us?'

'Excellent idea.' His father nodded approvingly. 'But after the drive this fire—' he held out his hands to the blazing warmth of the coal fire '—has much more appeal!' He grinned at his son.

'Take my coat from the hallway, Janette,' her mother told her. 'We don't want you to catch cold.'

She didn't want to go for a walk, had made no such suggestion in the first place, but with the four older people looking at her so expectantly she didn't seem to have a lot of choice in the matter. Not without appearing incredibly rude.

'I thought it best that you say what you have to say to me away from our parents,' Gabe bit out once they were outside in the crisp December air, walking over to the paddock where Jane had once kept her horse stabled.

She wasn't sure she could say anything to him, wasn't sure she could speak at all. She was still stunned by the fact that he was here at all. She had thought she would never see him again...

And how she had ached these last few days with that realisation!

How she ached now. But with quite a different emotion.

'Why, Gabe?' she finally managed to say.

He had been staring across at the bleak December landscape, a little snow having fallen in the night, leaving a crisp whiteness on everything. 'Why did I come here today with my parents?' he ground out. 'Because we were invited, Jane,' he responded harshly. 'It would have been rude not to have accepted.' He turned back to look over the paddock.

Jane looked up at his grim profile, his cheeks hollow, his jaw clenched. As if waiting for a blow...

She swallowed hard. 'I didn't mean that.' She shook her head. 'Why did you try to find me three years ago?' She felt that if she had the answer to that she might, just might, have the answer to the whole puzzle...

He looked down at her again, frowning slightly now. 'I thought you already knew the answer to that one,' he rasped scathingly. 'I was out to wreak vengeance, wasn't I? On a woman who had not only been deserted by her husband because of my wife, but had also been bombarded with reporters because of the scandal when the two of them died together in a car crash. Not only that, that woman had also lost her baby! That's the way it happened, isn't it, Jane?' he challenged disgustedly. 'You see, I've been doing some thinking of my own!' He shook his head. 'My conclusions aren't exactly pretty!'

She still stared up at him, couldn't seem to look away. She loved this man.

'I—' She moistened dry lips, swallowing hard. 'I could have been wrong—'

'Could have been?' Gabe turned fully towards her now, grasping her arms painfully. 'There's no "could have been" about it, Jane; if that's what you thought, you were wrong!' His eyes glittered dangerously, a nerve pulsing in his cheek. 'In fact, you're so damned far from the truth it's laughable. If I felt like laughing, that is,' he muttered grimly. 'Which I don't!'

She had done a lot of thinking herself over the last few days, and knew that somehow, some way, there was something wrong with what she had believed until two weeks ago, when she'd actually met Gabe for the first time. Maybe Gabe had been devastated by Jennifer's death, but the man she had come to know wouldn't blame anyone else for that death; he'd known the destructive streak that had motivated his wife better than anyone.

So if he hadn't wanted retribution all those years ago, what had he wanted...? It was that Jane wanted— needed—to know.

'Gabe, I was wrong,' she told him chokingly, putting

her hand on his arm, refusing to remove it even when she felt him flinch. 'I know that now. I know *you* now.'

He shook his head. 'No, you don't, Jane. Not really.'

And now she never would? Was that what he was saying?

She didn't want that, couldn't bear it if she were never to see him again after today. The past few days had been bad enough, but to go through that pain all over again...!

'Gabe, I'm trying to apologise. For what I thought,' she explained abruptly.

'Accepted.' He nodded tersely, his expression still hard. 'Can we go back inside now?' he added gratingly.

'Why are you helping my father, Gabe?' She refused to move, knowing that once they were back inside the house Gabe would become a remote stranger to her. And after telling him for days that that was what she wanted him to be it was now the last thing she wanted.

He gave a rueful grimace. 'So you know about that too now, hmm?' He nodded dismissively. 'Well, obviously I'm up to something underhand and malicious, entangling your father in some sort of plot—'

'Gabe!' Jane groaned her distress at his bitterness. 'I was wrong! I know I was wrong! I'm sorry. What else can I say?' She looked at him pleadingly.

He became very still now, looking down at her warily. 'What else do you want to say?'

So many things, but most of all, that she loved him. But how cautious she had, by necessity, been over the last three years of her life held her back from being quite that daring. What if he should throw that love back in her face?

She chewed on her bottom lip. 'I think your mother likes me,' she told him lightly, remembering what his mother's opinion of Jennifer had been.

His expression softened. 'You're right, she does,' he acknowledged dryly. 'But then, I knew she would,' he added enigmatically.

'Gabe, tell me why you tried to find me three years ago!' She tried again, because she was still sure this was the key to everything. 'Please, Gabe,' she pleaded as he looked grim once again.

'Do you have any idea what it's like to love someone so badly you can't even see straight?' he attacked viciously. 'So that you think of nothing else but that person, until they fill your whole world? Do you have any idea what it's like to love someone like that?' he groaned harshly. 'And then to have them disappear from your life as if they had never been, almost as if you had imagined them ever being there at all?' His hands were clenched at his sides, his face pale.

She was beginning to. Oh, yes, she was beginning to! And if he could still talk about his dead wife like this, still felt that way about her, then her own love for him was as worthless as ashes.

She drew in a deep breath. 'I'm sorry Jennifer died—'

'Jennifer? I'm not talking about Jennifer!' he dismissed incredulously. 'She was my wife, and as such I cared what happened to her, and could never actually bring myself to hate her—I felt pity for her more than anything. I hadn't loved her for years before she died. If I ever did,' he added bleakly. 'Compared with what I now know of love I believe I was initially fascinated by Jennifer, and then, after we were married, that fascination quickly turned to a rather sad affection. Beneath that surface selfishness was a very vulnerable woman, a woman who saw herself as being less than other women—I've already explained to you why that was. So you see, Jane, I felt sorry for Jennifer, I cared for her, but I was not in love with her. Before or after she died,' he said grimly.

'But—' Jane looked at him with puzzled eyes. If it wasn't Jennifer, then who was this mysterious woman he loved...? 'That perfect woman—the woman who evaporated, disappeared before your eyes.' She painfully recalled what he had told her of the woman he loved. The woman she had for so long assumed was Jennifer...

'What about her?' he echoed harshly.

Jane shook her head. 'Where is she? *Who* is she?'

Gabe looked down at her with narrowed eyes, his expression softening as he saw the look of complete bewilderment in her face. 'You really don't know, do you?' He shook his head self-derisively, moving away from her to lean back against the fence, the collar of his jacket turned up to keep out the worst of the cold. 'I was at a party one night—one of those endless parties that are impossible to enjoy, but you simply can't get away from. And then I looked across the crowded room—that well-worn cliché!—and there she was.'

Jane couldn't move, could barely breathe now.

Gabe was no longer looking at her, his thoughts all inwards as he recalled the past. 'I told myself not to be so stupid,' he continued harshly. 'Love didn't happen like that, in a moment—'

'At first sight.' Jane spoke hoarsely, remembering he had once asked her if she believed in the emotion. She had said a definite no!

'At first sight,' he echoed scornfully. 'But I couldn't stop watching this woman, couldn't seem to look anywhere else. And as I watched her I realised she wasn't just beautiful, she was gracious and warm too. She spoke to everybody there in the same warm way, and there was an elderly man there, who had been slightly drunk when he arrived, but instead of shying away from him as everyone else was she sat next to him, talking to him quietly, for over an hour. And by the time he left he was slightly less drunk and even managed to smile a little.'

'His wife had died the previous month,' Jane put in softly. 'That evening was the first time he had been out in company since her death. And people weren't shying away from him because he'd had slightly too much to drink; it was because they didn't know what to say to him, how to deal with his loss, and so they simply ignored him.' She remembered that night so well—it had been the last time she had gone anywhere with Paul, because, ironically enough, a few days later *he* had been dead.

Gabe nodded abruptly. 'I know that. I asked around who he was. Who you were. You were another man's wife!'

She was that perfect woman, the woman who had seemed to disappear, evaporate. And after the accident, after losing the baby, that was exactly what she had done!

Gabe had been in love with her three years ago! Not a man on a quest for vengeance, but a man on a quest for the woman he had fallen in love with at first sight at a party one night!

'You were another woman's husband,' she reminded him gruffly.

'Not by the time I came looking for you.' He shook his head firmly. 'The first time I saw you, I accept we were both married to other people, and in those circumstances I would never have come near you. I didn't come near you. And maybe I did act with indecent haste by trying to find you after our respective partners were killed,' he acknowledged grimly. 'But, as it happened, my worst nightmare came true.' He looked bleak. 'You had disappeared. And, no matter how I tried to find you, someone would put a wall up to block my way. After three months of coming up against those brick walls, of finally discovering that you had lost your baby because of what happened—'

'That was the reason you did a deal with Richard Warner rather than buy him out, wasn't it?' Jane said with certainty.

'A horror of history repeating itself?' Gabe nodded. 'It was too close to what happened to you three years ago.'

Jane gasped. 'You weren't responsible for my miscarriage—'

'Maybe I could have done something to stop Jennifer.' He shook his head. 'Who knows? I certainly didn't. So I tried to convince myself I had imagined you.' He sighed. 'I went back to the States, buried myself in my work, and told myself that Janette Granger was a myth, that even if I had finally got to meet you, speak to you, you would have hated me; that it was best to leave you as a dream, a mirage. The only trouble with dreams and mirages is that they transpose themselves over reality.' He grimaced.

'No normal woman can possibly live up to a dream one. And for me no woman ever has.'

He turned away abruptly, staring out across the empty paddock. 'When I met you again so suddenly two weeks ago. You were everything I had ever thought you were. And I was sure that you knew me too, but I thought— stupidly, I realise now—that if you could just get to know me, realise I wasn't a cold-hearted ogre, you might come to— Oh, never mind what I thought, Jane,' he rasped. 'I was wrong, so very wrong.'

'My name is Janette,' she put in softly, pointedly.

'Janie, if you prefer; it's always been my father's pet name for me.'

Gabe loved her. At least, he had loved her three years ago... Had the reality lived up to that dream?

He turned back to look at her. 'That night, at your apartment, I called you Janie...' he realised softly.

'You did,' she nodded. 'And I don't know what you're trying to do to help my father—'

'I'm putting him into Richard's company as his senior manager,' Gabe told her gently. 'Richard is good at PR work, and your father is good at the management level; together they should turn that company around in six months.' He swallowed hard. 'You were right about me; I had no idea of the financial difficulties your father had three years ago, of the debts he had to pay—'

'Paul's debts,' Jane put in hardly. 'My father did that for me. And what you're doing for him now has transformed his life—his and Mummy's. I could love you for just that alone,' she added shyly.

'Don't, Jane—'

'But I don't love you for that alone,' she continued determinedly, eyes very big in the paleness of her face as she looked up at him. 'I love you because you're warm and funny, caring and loving. And when you kiss me...!' She gave a self-conscious laugh.

'When I kiss you,' Gabe agreed throatily, 'I'm back to that first night I saw you; I can't think straight, can't see straight, all I know is you. With every part of me. Oh, Janie!'

She needed no further encouragement, flinging herself into his arms, both of them losing themselves in the sheer beauty of loving and being loved.

How long they remained like that Jane didn't know,

finally laughing gently against the warmth of his chest, where he had cradled her as if he would never let her go again.

'All we have to do now is find a way to explain to our respective parents that we're going to be married.' She chuckled softly. 'Considering my parents don't even realise we know each other—'

'Marriage, Janie?' Gabe looked down at her searchingly. 'You love me that much?'

And more. Marriage to Paul had been possession and pain; with Gabe it would be sharing and love. With Gabe, she had no doubts about making such a commitment. No doubts whatsoever.

'If you'll have me.' She nodded shyly, suddenly wondering if he was prepared to make such a commitment again after his disastrous marriage to Jennifer.

He let out a whoop of delight, picking her up to swing her round in the snow. 'Oh, I'll have you, Janette Smythe-Roberts, Janette Granger, Jane Smith. All of you! I love you, Janie, so very much.' He slowly lowered her to the snow-covered ground. 'And my parents already know how I feel about you, have known for some time that I left my heart behind in England three years ago,' he acknowledged ruefully. 'As for your own parents, they only want for you what will make you happy. And I certainly intend doing that! So will you marry me, Jane? Soon!' His arms tightened about her. 'It has to be soon!'

He had already waited long enough, his pleading expression told her. And so had she, she realised weakly. 'As soon as it can be arranged,' she assured him huskily. 'I can't wait for us to belong to each other. And my father was asking me only the other day when I was going to give him grandchildren…!' She looked up at Gabe hopefully.

'Children... *Our* children, Janie,' he groaned, his hands trembling as he held her. '*Soon*, Janie. Oh, yes, very soon!'

CHAPTER FOURTEEN

GOLD.

Bright, shiny, *warm* gold.

Her hair, returned to its natural colour for almost a year now, flowed like liquid gold over Gabe's fingers as he played with the silky tresses, his attention so intense he hadn't realised Jane had woken beside him in the bed and lay looking up at him.

It had been a good year—a year in which they had married and moved into a house of their own in London. Initially Jane's time had been filled with choosing the décor and furnishings, and soon—very soon!—her time was going to be filled with their son or daughter.

Being with Gabe, as his wife, was the deepest happiness Jane had ever known—falling asleep in his arms every night, waking still held in those strong arms, and spending their days busy in each other's company. Both sets of parents were constant visitors, eager for the birth of their first grandchild. As Jane and Gabe were.

'Good morning, my love.' She greeted her husband huskily, warmed by the pleasure that lit his face as he realised she was awake.

He kissed her lingeringly on the lips. 'I've just been wondering what I ever found to do with my time before I had you to look at and love,' he admitted ruefully. 'You're so beautiful, Jane,' he told her shakily.

She laughed softly, reaching up to gently touch his cheek. 'At the moment I look like a baby whale!'

His hand moved to rest possessively on the swell of

her body that was their unborn child. 'To me you're beautiful.'

And she knew he meant it, that he had enjoyed every aspect of her pregnancy, been a part of all of it, as far as he was able. And since Felicity and Richard's son Thom had been born six months ago, the other couple now close friends who visited often, Gabe had been practising changing nappies, much to baby Thom's disgust.

'You were very restless last night, darling.' Gabe frowned down at her concernedly now. 'Do you feel okay?'

Jane grinned up at him. 'As okay as I can be in the early stages of labour,' she informed him lightly, knowing that the slight cramps she had had in her stomach the evening before had deepened during the night, although not seriously enough yet for her to need to go to hospital, which was why she had been napping on and off during the night, preparing herself for the much heavier labour she was positive was imminent.

Gabe shot out of bed so quickly Jane could only lie and stare at him, moving up to lean on one elbow to watch him as he raced around the bedroom, throwing on his own clothes, before puling her own out of the adjoining wardrobe and laying them down on the bed.

'Gabe...?' She finally stopped his rushing about. 'It's going to be hours yet—'

He came to an abrupt halt, sitting down on the side of the bed, gently clasping her shoulders. 'I'm not taking any chances with you, Jane,' he told her emotionally. 'If anything should happen to you—'

Jane placed her fingertips lightly against his lips. 'Nothing is going to happen to me,' she assured him confidently. 'We fell in love with each other against all the odds; nothing could possibly happen to part us now,' she said with conviction, sure in her own heart that they were meant to be together. Always.

'I love you so much, Jane,' he choked. 'My life would be empty without you!'

'And mine without you. But that isn't going to happen, Gabe.' She was absolutely positive about this, felt sure they were going to grow old together. 'Nothing is going to happen in the next few hours except we're going to have our own darling little baby.' She gave him a glowing smile. 'But perhaps you're right about going to the hospital now.' She began her breathing exercises as a much stronger contraction took her breath away. 'I think the baby has decided that today would be a good time to be born!'

And six hours later, when their daughter Ami was born, with Jane's golden hair and Gabe's aqua-blue eyes, they knew that their world was complete.

'She's gorgeous, Jane.' Gabe gazed down wonderingly at their tiny daughter, each tiny feature perfect. 'I can't believe you're both mine.' He shook his head.

'Believe it, Gabe,' Jane told him emotionally.

As she believed.

In Gabe.

In their marriage.

In their for ever...

If you enjoyed what you just read,
then we've got an offer you can't resist!

Take 2 bestselling love stories FREE!

Plus get a FREE surprise gift!

ROMANTIC FANTASIES COME ALIVE WITH

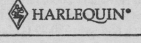

HARLEQUIN®

INTIMACIES

Harlequin is turning up the heat with
this seductive collection!

Experience the passion as the heroes and heroines explore
their deepest desires, their innermost secrets. Get lost in
these tantalizing stories that will leave you wanting more!

Available in November at your favorite retail outlet:

OUT OF CONTROL by Candace Schuler
NIGHT RHYTHMS by Elda Minger
SCANDALIZED! by Lori Foster
PRIVATE FANTASIES by Janelle Denison

You're not going to believe this offer!

In October and November 2000, buy any two Harlequin or Silhouette books and save $10.00 off future purchases, or buy any three and save $20.00 off future purchases!

Just fill out this form and attach 2 proofs of purchase (cash register receipts) from October and November 2000 books and Harlequin will send you a coupon booklet worth a total savings of $10.00 off future purchases of Harlequin and Silhouette books in 2001. Send us 3 proofs of purchase and we will send you a coupon booklet worth a total savings of $20.00 off future purchases.

Saving money has never been this easy.

I accept your offer! Please send me a coupon booklet:

Name: _____

Address: _____ City: _____

State/Prov.: _____ Zip/Postal Code: _____

Optional Survey!

In a typical month, how many Harlequin or Silhouette books would you buy <u>new</u> at retail stores?

☐ Less than 1 ☐ 1 ☐ 2 ☐ 3 to 4 ☐ 5+

Which of the following statements best describes how you <u>buy</u> Harlequin or Silhouette books? Choose one answer only that <u>best</u> describes you.

☐ I am a regular buyer and reader
☐ I am a regular reader but buy only occasionally
☐ I only buy and read for specific times of the year, e.g. vacations
☐ I subscribe through Reader Service but also buy at retail stores
☐ I mainly borrow and buy only occasionally
☐ I am an occasional buyer and reader

Which of the following statements best describes how you <u>choose</u> the Harlequin and Silhouette series books you buy <u>new</u> at retail stores? By "series," we mean books within a particular line, such as *Harlequin PRESENTS* or *Silhouette SPECIAL EDITION*. Choose one answer only that <u>best</u> describes you.

☐ I only buy books from my favorite series
☐ I generally buy books from my favorite series but also buy books from other series on occasion
☐ I buy some books from my favorite series but also buy from many other series regularly
☐ I buy all types of books depending on my mood and what I find interesting and have no favorite series

Please send this form, along with your cash register receipts as proofs of purchase, to:
In the U.S.: Harlequin Books, P.O. Box 9057, Buffalo, NY 14269
In Canada: Harlequin Books, P.O. Box 622, Fort Erie, Ontario L2A 5X3
(Allow 4-6 weeks for delivery) Offer expires December 31, 2000.

PHQ4002